Oliver Goldsmith

Essays and Criticisms By Dr. Goldsmith - With an Account of the Author

Vol. II

Oliver Goldsmith

Essays and Criticisms By Dr. Goldsmith - With an Account of the Author
Vol. II

ISBN/EAN: 9783337279363

Printed in Europe, USA, Canada, Australia, Japan

Cover: Foto ©Andreas Hilbeck / pixelio.de

More available books at **www.hansebooks.com**

ESSAYS

AND

CRITICISMS,

BY DR. GOLDSMITH;

WITH

AN ACCOUNT

OF

THE AUTHOR.

IN THREE VOLUMES.

VOL. II.

NOW FIRST COLLECTED.

𝕷𝖔𝖓𝖉𝖔𝖓:

PRINTED FOR J. JOHNSON, ST. PAUL'S CHURCH-YARD.

M.DCC.XCVIII.

PREFACE.

IT was the fate of the ingenious Author of the ESSAYS and CRITICISMS, now firſt collectively offered to the Public, to begin his literary career, unknown and unpatronized, laboriouſly employing himſelf to provide for the exigencies of the paſſing day; and during that period of penury and diſtreſs, ſcattering over the periodical publications of the times, works of merit, enough to confer celebrity on any name whoſe owner had the advantage of being known to the world. Works which, from the obſcurity of the author, were neglected

a 3   and

and left to perifh amidft the rubbifh with
which they were furrounded.

GENIUS, however, in a country like
Great Britain, cannot long be depreffed.
That of GOLDSMITH at length triumphed
over the difficulties of his fituation. By
flow degrees he forced himfelf into notice. His talents were allowed; enquiry
was made after his early performances;
and fome of them he was induced to re-
vife, correct, and publifh in a Volume *
himfelf. To thofe ESSAYS ample juftice
has been rendered; and fuch is public
caprice, thofe who were blind to the ex-
cellencies of an obfcure author, while
ftruggling for notice, and even for exift-

* This Volume of ESSAYS was publifhed by Dr.
GOLDSMITH in 1765, and forms the firft Volume of
this Publication.

ence, were foon compelled to applaud the flaſhes of wit; the happy ſtrokes of humour; the accurate obſervation on life and manners, and the ſuccefsful delineation of character, which afterwards ſhone, forth with acknowledged ſplendour, in the admirable Comedies of " The Goodnatured Man," and " She Stoops to Conquer."

BUT though the Essays, publiſhed by Dr. Goldsmith himſelf, were received by the world as the genuine efforts of genius, they were ſtill but a ſelection. Many pieces of undoubted excellence were known to be omitted, and ſome which were ſuſpected to be of his compoſition could not be certainly aſcertained. Theſe circumſtances occaſioned enquiry, and enquiry was the means of bringing to

light

light what otherwife would not have been
known. The late Mr. THOMAS WRIGHT,
Printer, a man of literary obfervation and
experience, had, during his conneƈtion
with thofe periodical publications, in
which the early works of Dr. GOLD-
SMITH were originally contained, carefully marked the feveral compofitions of
the different writers, as they were delivered to him to print. Being therefore,
it was fuppofed, the only perfon able to
feparate the genuine performances of Dr.
GOLDSMITH from thofe of other writers,
in thefe mifcellaneous colleƈtions, it became the wifh of feveral admirers of the
Author of The Traveller and Deferted
Village, that his authentic writings fhould
no longer be blended with either doubtful or fpurious pieces. Mr. WRIGHT
was therefore recommended and prevailed

upon

upon to print the prefent Selection, which he had juft completed at the time of his death.

To expatiate on the merit of the prefent Collection, or the Author of it, would be a wafte of time. His reputation is eftablifhed beyond the reach of criticifm, and it is prefumed will fuffer no diminution from the prefent Volumes, which the difcerning Reader will perceive bear evident marks of authenticity, and prove themfelves to be the undoubted works of Dr. GOLDSMITH.

LIFE

DR. GOLDSMITH.

OLIVER GOLDSMITH was the third fon of the Rev.
Charles Goldfmith, a divine of great refpectabi-
lity, though but in narrow circumftances. He was born
at Elphin, in the county of Rofcommon, in the kingdom
of Ireland, 29th November, in the year 1731*, and was
inftructed in the claffics, at the fchool of Mr. Hughes.
On the 11th of June, 1744, he was admitted a Sizer
of Trinity College, Dublin, under the tuition of Dr.
Radcliffe, where he was contemporary with Mr. Edmund Burke. At college he exhibited no fpecimens
of that genius which diftinguifhed him in his maturer
years. According to his own whimfical account of
himfelf, " he made no great figure in mathematics,
which was a ftudy much in repute there, yet he could
turn an ode of Horace into Englifh better than any of
them." On the 27th of February, 1749, O. S. (two
years after the regular time), he obtained the degree
of Bachelor of Arts. At this period of his life he
turned his thoughts to the profeffion of phyfic; and

* So fays his Epitaph. Other accounts place his birth, and
not without probability, in 1729.

a 6   after

after attending fome courfes of anatomy in Dublin, he proceeded to Edinburgh, in the year 1751, where he purfued the ftudy of the feveral branches of medicine, under the different profeffors in that univerfity. At this period of his life, the fame want of thought and circumfpeۂion, and the fame heedlefs beneficence governed, that in his latter years continued to involve him in difficulties. Imprudently engaging to pay a confiderable fum of money for a fellow ftudent, who failed to exonerate him from the demand, he found himfelf under the neceffity of haftily quitting Scotland, to avoid the horrours of a jail.

Sunderland was the place in which he took refuge, and there he arrived in the beginning of the year 1754. His fudden flight had left him no means of providing for his prefent wants, and he was driven to the greateft extremity. It was at this period, it is imagined, that he was reduced to an embarraffment, which will be beft related in the words of the perfon who originally gave the anecdote to the public*.

" Upon his firft going to England he was in fuch diftrefs, that he would have gladly become an ufher to a country fchool; but fo deftitute was he of friends to

* A Philofophical Survey of the South of Ireland, in a Series of Letters to John Watkinfon, M. D. Dublin, 8vo. 1788, p. 286.

recommend

recommend him, that he could not without difficulty obtain even this low department. The master of the school scrupled to employ him, without some testimonial of his paſt life. GOLDSMITH referred him to his tutor at college for a character; but all this while he went under a feigned name. From this reſource, therefore, one would think that little in his favour could be even hoped for; but he only wanted to ſerve a preſent exigency—an uſherſhip was not his object.

" IN this ſtrait he writes a letter to Dr. Radcliffe, imploring him, as he tendered the welfare of an old pupil, not to anſwer a letter which he would probably receive the ſame poſt with his own, from the ſchoolmaſter. He added, that he had good reaſons for concealing, both from him and the reſt of the world, his name, and the real ſtate of his caſe: eveiy circumſtance of which he promiſed to communicate upon ſome future occaſion. His tutor, embarraſſed enough before to know what anſwer he ſhould give, reſolved at laſt to give none. And thus was poor GOLDSMITH ſnatched from between the horns of his preſent dilemma, and ſuffered to drag on a miſerable life for a few probationary months.

" IT was not till after his return to London, from his rambles over great part of the world, and after having got ſome ſure footing on this ſlippery globe, that he at length wrote to Dr. Radcliffe, to thank him for

for not anfwering the fchoolmafter's letter, and to fulfil his promife of giving the hiftory of the whole tranfac-tion. It contained a comical narrative of his adven-tures, from his leaving Ireland to that time," It is to be regretted that accident has fince deftroyed this narra-tive, which the gentleman to whom it was written, ad-mired more than any part of our author's works.

BUT although Dr. GOLDSMITH had efcaped from Scotland into England, he could not fecure himfelf from the fangs of the law. The vigilance of his cre-ditor, a tailor, followed him, and he was arrefted for the money, on account of which he had become fecu-rity. From this difficulty he was releafed by the friend-fhip of Mr. Laughlin Maclane and Dr. Sleigh, who were then at the college of Edinburgh. As foon as he was at liberty, he took his paffage on board a Dutch fhip to Rotterdam, from whence, after a fhort ftay, he proceeded to Bruffels. He then vifited a great part of Flanders; and after paffing fome time at Strafbourg and Louvain, at which laft place he obtained a degree of Bachelor in Phyfic, he accompanied an Englifh gentle-man to Geneva.

IT is faid, on unqueftionable authority, that our in-genious author performed the greater part of his travels on foot; and he himfelf alludes to this circumftance in one of his early works. " Countries," fays he, " wear different appearances to travellers of different circum-ftances.

ftances. A man who is whirled through Europe in a poft-chaife, ahd the pilgrim who walks the grand tour on foot, will form very different conclufions.—*Haud in-expertus loquor.*" It has been afferted, that he was en-abled to purfue his travels, partly by demanding at univerfities to enter the lifts as a difputant, by which, according to the cuftom of many of them, he was en-titled to the premium of a crown, when, luckily for him, his challenge was not accepted ; fo that, as it has been obferved, he difputed his paffage through Eu-rope.

He had left England ill provided with money ; but being at that time of a rambling difpofition, and having probably no fettled fcheme of life, he neither forefaw, nor feared, any difficulties. He poffeffed alfo a body capable of fuftaining every fatigue, and a mind not eafily terrified by danger. Thus qualified, he formed the defign of feeing the manners of different countries. He had acquired fome knowledge of the French lan-guage, and of mufic ; he played alfo on the German flute, which he found a very ufeful accomplifhment, as at times it afforded him the means of fubfiftence, which all his other qualities would have failed to acquire for him. His learning, though not profound, produced him an hofpitable reception at moft of the religious houfes that he vifited ; and his mufic made him wel-come to the peafants of Flanders and Germany. " Whenever I approached a peafant's houfe towards nightfall,"

nightfall," he ufed to fay, " I. played one of my moft merry tunes, and that generally procured me not only a lodging, but fubfiftence for the next day ; but in truth," his conftant expreffion, " I muft own, whenever I attempted to entertain perfons of a higher rank, they always thought my performance odious, and never made me any return for my endeavours to pleafe them."

On his arrival at Geneva, it is faid he was recommended as travelling tutor to a young man of mean birth and fordid difpofition, who, after he had arrived at years of maturity, unexpectedly came into poffeffion of a confiderable fortune. With this perfon our author proceeded to the South of France, where a difagreement arofe between the tutor and pupil, which ended in their parting from each other. Once more our ill-fated traveller was left to encounter the difficulties of a friendlefs ftranger in a foreign country. He had by this time fatisfied his curiofity, and accordingly bent his fteps towards England, where he arrived fome time about the year 1757.

His fituation was now altered, but not improved. He was ftill a ftranger, and ftill deftitute. " The world was all before him," but the means of prefent fubfiftence was not eafily to be obtained. He applied to feveral apothecaries to be received as a journeyman ; but his broad Irifh accent, and uncouth appearance, operated

operated againft his reception. In this forlorn ftate he was at length obliged to fubmit to the humble condition of an affiftant in the laboratory of a chemift near Fifh-ftreet Hill. From this drudgery he was releafed by the kindnefs of his friend Dr. Sleigh, who received him into his family, and undertook to fupport him, until fome means could be devifed for his maintenance. In a fhort time he accepted the employment of ufher to a boarding-fchool, kept by Dr. Milner, a diffenting teacher, at Peckham. Though this ftation, when viewed in its proper light, can be efteemed neither difhonourable nor difgraceful, yet, it is remarkable, it was the only one which GOLDSMITH fhrunk from the recollection of, when he attained a more profperous ftate.

IT is imagined, that while he was ufher to Dr. Milner, he firft engaged in the purfuits of literature. The earlieft performance by him, now to be difcovered, is, " The Memoirs of a Proteftant, condemned to the Galleys of France for his Religion. Written by himfelf. Tranflated from the Original, juft publifhed at the Hague, by James Willington;" 1758, two volumes, 12mo, for which Mr. Edward Dilly paid him twenty guineas. In 1759 appeared " An Enquiry into the prefent State of Polite Learning in Europe ;" and in October of the fame year he began " The Bee," a weekly publication, which ceafed at the end of eight numbers.

numbers. In the next year he became known to Dr. Smollett, who was then publifhing " The Britifh Magazine ;" and for that work our author compofed feveral of the effays, which he afterwards collected into the volume already mentioned, as well as fome of thofe inferted in the prefent volumes. He alfo engaged as an affiftant in the Critical Review; and it is believed wrote fome articles in the Monthly Review.

In the commencement of his literary career, he de-termined to obferve the rules of economy very rigidly, and with that view took a lodging in Green-arbour Court, in the Old Bailey, where the greater part of his moft fuccefsful pieces were written. He had been introduced to Mr. Newbery, a man who truly deferved the eulogium beftowed by Dr. Warburton on the book-fellers in general, as " one of the beft judges and re-warders of merit," by whom he. was employed to write in the Public Ledger the Chinefe Letters, afterwards collected under the title of " The Citizen of the World;" and foon after he obtained the friendfhip of Dr. Samuel Johnfon, who encouraged him in his pur-fuits, applauded his exertions, and occafionally affifted him with his advice.

Our author, however, did not foon emerge from obfcurity. He continued in his humble abode in Green-arbour Court, until about the middle of the year

year 1762, when he removed to a handfome fet of chambers in the Middle Temple. His name was ftill but little known, except among the bookfellers, until the year 1765, when his genius difplayed itfelf in its full vigour by the publication of " The Traveller, or a Profpect of Society ;" a poem began in Switzerland, and which was revifed by Dr. Johnfon; who pronounced this eulogium on it, " that there had not been fo fine a Poem fince Pope's time."

In the year 1767, our author, who had now affumed the title of Doctor, made his firft, and, probably, his only effort, towards obtaining a permanent eftablifhment. On the death of Mr. Mace, Grefham Profeffor of Civil Law, he became a candidate to fucceed him ; but without fuccefs. In 1768, his firft play, The Good-Natured Man, was acted at Covent Garden, with lefs approbation than it deferved. Dr. Johnfon's opinion of this performance was, that it was the beft comedy that had appeared fince The Provoked Hufband ; and that there had not been of late any fuch character on the ftage as that of Croaker. In the fucceeding year he had the honorary Profefforfhip of Hiftory in the Royal Academy conferred on him ; and in this year his beautiful poem, " The Deferted Village," was firft printed.

The eftimation in which he was held by the bookfellers

fellers was at this time fo great, that he was folicited to
engage in a variety of works, fome of which, it cannot
be denied, were executed in a hafty and flovenly manner. His reputation however was but little diminifhed
to the end of his life. His emoluments were very
great ; and had he poffeffed only a fmall portion of
prudence, he might have enfured that independence,
the want of which embittered his latter days, and contributed in fome meafure to fhorten his life.

His generofity, not to call it profufion, was without bounds ; and he had conftantly a fet of miferable
dependants, whofe wants he fupplied, even to the dif-
treffing himfelf. He had alfo unfortunately contracted
a habit of gaming, with the arts of which he was very
little acquainted ; and confequently became the prey
of fome who were unprincipled enough to take advantage of his ignorance. An habitual careleffnefs
with refpect to money matters, at all times appears to
have been his predominant failing. Though, as already
obferved, the emoluments arifing from his writings
were very great, yet his income bore no proportion to
his expences. He became embarraffed in his circumftances, and in confequence uneafy, fretful, and peevifh.
To this was added a violent ftrangury, with which he
was fome years afflicted, and which, with other mif-
fortunes, brought on a kind of habitual defpondency.
In this ftate he was attacked by a nervous fever, which,
being

being improperly treated, terminated in his diffolution the 4th of April, 1774, in the forty-third year of his age. It was firft intended by his friends to bury him. in Weftminfter Abbey; his pall was to have been fupported by Lord Shelburne, Lord Louth, Sir Jofhua Reynolds, the Honourable Mr. Beauclerc, Mr. Edmund Burke, and Mr. Garrick; but a flight infpection into his affairs fhowed the impropriety of that defign. He was therefore privately interred, in the burial ground belonging to the Temple; when Mr. Hugh Kelly, Meffrs. John and Robert Day, Mr. Palmer, Mr. Etherington, and Mr. Hawes, gentlemen, who had been his friends in life, attended his corps as mourners, and paid the laft tribute to his memory.

Dr. Johnson's charaĉter of Goldsmith, as an author, a few years after his death, is highly honourable to him. " He was," fays that admirable writer, " a man of fuch variety of powers, and fuch felicity of performance, that he always feemed to do beft, that which he was doing; a man who had the art of being minute without tedioufnefs, and general without confufion; whofe language was copious without exuberance, exaĉt without conftraint, and eafy without weaknefs."

Mr. Boswell has alfo pourtrayed our author; and fome of his traits of his charaĉter will be readily recognized

nized by his furviving friends. " No man had the art
of difplaying with more advantage, as a writer, whatever literary acquifition he made.—*Nihil quod tetigit non
ornavit.*—His mind refembled a fertile, but thin foil.
There was a quick, but not a ftrong vegetation, of
whatever chanced to be thrown upon it. No deep root
could be ftruck. The oak of the foreft did not grow
there; but the elegant fhrubbery, and the fragrant
parterre, appeared in gay fucceffion. It has been generally circulated and believed, that he was a mere fool
in converfation; but, in truth, this has been greatly
exaggerated. He had, no doubt, a more than common fhare of that hurry of ideas which we often find in
his countrymen, and which fometimes produces a laugh-
able confufion in expreffing them. He was very much
what the French call *un etourdi*; and from vanity, and
an eager defire of being confpicuous where-ever he was,
he frequently talked carelefsly, without knowledge of
the fubject, or even without thought. His perfon was
fhort; his countenance coarfe and vulgar; his deportment that of a fcholar, awkwardly affecting the eafy
gentleman. Thofe who were in any way diftinguifhed,
excited envy in him to fo ridiculous an excefs, that the
inftances of it are hardly credible."—" He, I am
afraid, had no fettled fyftem of any fort, fo that his
conduct muft not be ftrictly fcrutinized; but his affections were focial and generous; and when he had
money, he gave it away very liberally."

T&

To thefe accounts, we fhall add the following pleafant defcription of our author, by the fprightly pen of
David Garrick.

HERE, Hermes, fays Jove, who with nectar was mellow,
Go, fetch me fome clay—I will make an odd fellow.
Right and wrong fhall be jumbled ; much gold, and
    fome drofs ;
Without caufe be he pleafed, without caufe be he orofs :
Be fure, as 1 work, to throw in contradictions ;
A great lover of truth, yet a mind turn'd to fictions.
Now mix thefe ingredients, which, warm'd in the
    baking,
Turn to learning and gaming, religion and raking ;
With the love of a wench, let his writings be chafte,
Tip his tongue with ftrange matter, his pen with fine
    tafte.
That the rake and the poet o'er all may prevail,
Set fire to his head, and fet fire to his tail :
For the joy of each fex on the world I'll beftow it,
This fcholar, rake, chriftian, dupe, gamefter, and poet.
Though a mixture fo odd, he fhall merit great fame,
And among brother mortals be GOLDSMITH his name.
When on earth this ftrange meteor no more fhall appear,
You, Hermes, fhall fetch him, to make us fport here.

A FEW years after his death a monument, by Nolli-
kens, was erected in Weftminfter Abbey, by a collection made by his friends ; and upon it is infcribed
                                                    the

the following epitaph, written by Dr. Samuel Johnson :

OLIVARII GOLDSMITH
POETÆ, PHYSICI, HISTORICI,
QUI NULLUM FERE SCRIBENDI GENUS
NON TETIGIT,
NULLUM QUOD TETIGIT NON ORNAVIT;
SIVE RISUS ESSENT MOVENDI,
SIVE LACRYMÆ,
AFFECTUUM POTENS, AT LENIS DOMINATOR;
INGENIO SUBLIMIS, VIVIDUS, VERSATILIS;
ORATIONE GRANDIS, NITIDUS, VENUSTUS;
HOC MONUMENTO MEMORIAM COLUIT
SODALIUM AMOR,
AMICORUM FIDES,
LECTORUM VENERATIO.
NATUS HIBERNIA, FORNEIÆ LONFORDIENSIS
IN LOCO CUI NOMEN PALLAS,
NOV. XXIX. MDCCXXXI.
EBLANÆ LITERIS INSTITUTUS,
OBIIT LONDINI,
APR. IV. MDCCLXXIV.

AN

AN

ORIGINAL LETTER

OF

DR. GOLDSMITH.

TO

ROBERT BRAYNTON, Esq. Ballymahon, Ireland.

Edinburgh, Sept. 26, 1753.

MY DEAR BOB,

HOW many good excufes (and you know I was
ever good at an excufe) might I call up to vin-
dicate my paft fhameful filence!—I might tell how I
wrote a long letter at my firft coming hither, and
feem vaftly angry at my not receiving an anfwer; I
might allege that bufinefs (with bufinefs you know I
was always peftered) had never given me time to finger
a pen;—but I fupprefs thefe, and twenty more equally
plaufible and as eafily invented, fince they might be
attended with a flight inconvenience of being known
to be lies. Let me then fpeak truth: an hereditary
indolence (I have it from the mother's fide) has hi-
therto prevented my writing to you, and ftill prevents
my writing at leaft twenty-five letters more, due to

VOL. II.   b   my

my friends in Ireland. No turnfpit dog gets up into his wheel with more reluctance than I fit down to write; yet no dog ever loved the roaft meat he turns better than I do him I now addrefs.—Yet what fhall I fay now I am enter'd ? Shall I tire you with a de-fcription of this unfruitful country, where I muft lead you over their hills all brown with heath, or their vallies fcarce able to feed a rabbit ?—Man alone feems to be the only creature who has arrived to the natural fize in this poor foil.—Every part of the country pre-fents the fame difmal landfcape : no grove nor brook lend their mufic to cheer the ftranger, or make the inhabitants forget their poverty :—yet, with all thefe difadvantages to call him down to humility, a Scotch-man is one of the proudeft things alive.—The poor have · pride ever ready to relieve them :—if mankind fhould happen to defpife them, they are mafters of their own admiration, and *that* they can plentifully be-ftow on themfelves.

FROM their pride and poverty, as I take it, refults one advantage this country enjoys, namely, the gentle-men are much better bred than amongft us.—No fuch character here as our fox-hunters; and they have ex-preffed great furprize when I informed them that fome men in Ireland of 1000l. a year fpend their whole lives in running after a hare, drinking to be drunk, and getting every girl, that will let them, with child : and truly, if fuch a being, equipped in his hunting drefs,

came

eame among a circle of Scotch gentry, they would
behold him with the fame aftonifhment that a countryman would King George on horfeback. The men
here have generally high cheek-bones, and are lean
and fwarthy, fond of action, dancing in particular.
Though, now I mention dancing, let me fay fomething
of their balls, which are very frequent here.—When a
ftranger enters the dancing-hall, he fees one end of the
room taken up with the ladies, who fit difmally in a
groupe by themfelves; on the other end ftands their
penfive partners, that are to be; but no more inter-
coufe between the fexes, than there is between two
countries at war:—the ladies, indeed, may ogle, and
the gentlemen figh, but an embargo is laid on any
clofer commerce. At length, to interrupt hoftilities,
the lady directrefs, or intendant, or what you will,
pitches on a gentleman and lady to walk a minuet,
which they perform with a formality that approaches
defpondence. After five or fix couple have thus walked
the gauntlet, all ftand up to country dances, each gentleman furnifhed with a partner from the aforefaid lady
directrefs, fo they dance much and fay nothing, and
thus concludes our affembly. I told a Scotch gentleman, that fuch profound filence refembled the ancient
proceffion of the Roman matrons in honour of Ceres:
and the Scotch gentleman told me (and, faith, I believe he was right) that I was a very great pedant for
my pains.—Now I'm come to the ladies, and to fhew
that I love Scotland, and every thing that belongs to

b 2   fe

fo charming a country, I infift on it, and will give him
leave to break my head that denies it, that the Scotch
ladies are ten thoufand times handfomer and finer than
the Irifh :—to be fure now I fee your fifters Betty and
Peggy vaftly furprized at my partiality, but tell them
flatly, I don't value them, or their fine fkins, or eyes,
ₙor good fenfe, or ————, a potatoe ; for I fay it, and
will maintain it, and, as a convincing proof (I'm in a
very great paffion) of what I affert, the Scotch ladies -
fay it themfelves.   But, to be lefs ferious, where will
you find a language fo pretty become a pretty mouth,
as the broad Scotch ? and the women here fpeak it in
its higheft purity ; for inftance, teach one of their
young ladies to pronounce—" Whoar wull I gong"—
with a becoming widenefs of mouth, and I'll lay my
life they will wound every hearer.   We have no fuch
character here as a coquet ; but, alas ! how many en·
vious prudes !—Some days ago I walked into my Lord
Kilkoubry's (dont't be furprized, my Lord is but a
glover), when the Duchefs of Hamilton (that fair who
facrificed her beauty to ambition, and her inward peace
to a title and gilt equipage) paffed by in her chariot ;
her battered hufband, or, more properly, the guardian
of her charms, fat by her fide.   Strait envy began, in
the fhape of no lefs than three ladies, who fat with me,
to find faults in her faultlefs form :—" For my part,"
fays the firft, " I think, what I always thought, that
the Duchefs has too much red in her complexion."—
" Madam, I'm of your opinion," fays the fecond,
and

" and I think her face has a palifh caft, too much on
the delicate order."—" And let me tell you," adds
the third lady, whofe mouth was puckered up to the
fize of an iffue, " that the Duchefs has fine lips, but
fhe wants a mouth."—At this, every lady drew up her
mouth as if fhe was going to pronounce the letter P.
——But how ill, my Bob, does it become me, to
ridicule women with whom I have fcarce any corre-
fpondence!—There are, 'tis certain, handfome women
here; and 'tis as certain, there are handfome men to
keep them company.—An ugly and a poor man is
fociety for himfelf: and fuch fociety the world lets me
enjoy in great abundance.—Fortune has given you circumftances, and nature a perfon, to look charming in
the eyes of the fair world. Nor do I envy my dear
Bob fuch bleffings, while I may fit down and laugh at
the world, and at myfelf, the moft ridiculous object in
it.—But I begin to grow fplenetic ; and, perhaps, the
fit may continue till 1 receive an anfwer to this. I
know you can't fend news from B. Mahon, but, fuch
as it is fend it all ; every thing you write will be agreeable and entertaining to me. Has George Conway
put up a fign yet ; or John Finecly left off drinking
drams ; or Tom Allen got a new wig? But I leave to
your own choice what to write.—While OLIVER
GOLDSMITH lives, know you have a friend!

P.S. GIVE my fincereft regards (not compliments,
do you mind) to your agreeable family; and give my
fervice

fervice to my mother, if you fee her, for, as you exprefs it in Ireland, I have a fneaking kindnefs for her
ftill.

DIRECT to me—Student in Phyfic, in Edinburgh.

ESSAY

CONTENTS.

VOL. II.

E S S A Y S.

E S S A Y I.

WRITTEN IN THE YEAR M.DCC.LX.

WE know not a character of antiquity which can be produced as a rival to that of the present Minister *.

His eloquence, integrity, and zeal for the interests of the commonwealth, may have been equalled by several individuals both of Greece and Rome ; but the vigour, sagacity, and success with which he has exerted those qualities, are unprecedented ; and his universal popularity in a free

---

* The Right Hon. W. PITT, Esq. then one of his MAJESTY's PRINCIPAL SECRETARIES of STATE, and afterwards created EARL OF CHATHAM, father of the present CHANCELLOR OF THE EXCHEQUER.

VOL. II.   B   state,

flate, which had been long divided by inveterate factions, is altogether without example.

WERE we obliged to find a parallel between him and fome diftinguifhed character of the ancient republics, we fhould compare him to the Two Brothers the GRACCHI, the illuftrious advocates of the Roman people, and the moft fhining orna-ments of a polifhed commonwealth. We would compare him to both the Brothers, becaufe the virtues and accomplifhments of both feem united in his character.

TIBERIUS GRACCHUS and CAIUS GRACCHUS were of the Sempronian family, which, though Plebeian, was eminent, worthy, and honourable, and allied to the moft noble houfes of Rome. Both Brothers were actuated by the fame warm zeal for the intereft of their fellow-citizens ; and fo extraordinary were their talents, that, had they flourifhed at tne fame period of time, their united endeavours muft have furmounted all oppofition : but Caius, being the junior by nine years, could not co-operate with his brother Tiberius in the great fcheme he had projected in behalf of the common people ; and he afterwards adopted his plan without fuccefs.   Each made his efforts fe-parately, and both perifhed in the fame attempt, through the jealoufy and refentment of the patri-
ci ans.

cians. Their enemies accufed them of ambition :
but * the imputation was unjuft. In reviving
the Licinian law for the divifion of lands, they
were folely animated and influenced by a principle
of patriot humanity, which indeed glowed to a degree of enthufiafm. ...,   ...

VELLEIUS PATERCULUS, that, elegant fyco-
phant of arbitrary power, is forced to acknowledge,
that, bating their fuppofed defign againft the conftitution of their country, their morals were unblemifhed, and their lives irreproachable. He
owns their genius was fublime, and that their engagements were facred : in a word, that they were
adorned with all the virtues that human nature, in
its greateft perfection, could acquire or poffefs.
Yet there was an effential difference in the characters of thefe two celebrated Roman patriots.
Tiberius was mild and compofed, of a winning
addrefs and gentle difpofition : when he harangued
in public, he feemed to folicit, and indeed to fe-

* ὁ δὲ ἀδελφὸς αὐτῶ Γάι⊙- ἔν τινι βιϐλίῳ γέγραφεν, εἰς
Νομαντίαν πορευόμενον διὰ τῆς Τυῤῥηνιας τὸν Τιϐέριον, και
τὴν ἐρημίαν τῆς χώρας ὁρῶντα, καὶ τὰς γεωργᾶντας ἢ νέμοντας,
οἰκέτας· ἐπεισάκλᾳς καὶ βαρϐάρᾳς· τότε πρῶτον ἐπὶ νᾶν βαλέσθαι
τὴν μυρίων κακων ἄρξασαν αὐτοῖς πολιτείαν. Τὴν δὲ πλείρην
αὐτὸς· ὁ δῆμ⊙- ὁρμὴν καὶ φιλοτιμίαν ἐξῆψε, προκαλέμεν⊙·
διὰ γραμμάτων αὐτὸν ἐν ροαῖς· καὶ τοίχοις καὶ μνήμασι
γραφομενων, ἀναλαϐεῖν τοῖς πένησι τὴν δημοσίαν χώραν.

ΠΛΟΥΤΑΡΧ. ΤΙΒ. ΓΡΑΚΧ.

duce

duce the applause of his audience, by artful arguments and pathetic images : his elocution was soft
and infinuating : he endeavoured to pleafe, in order to perfuade. Caius was more open, bold, and
impetuous.   He poffeffed an irrefiftible energy of
eloquence, enforced with fublime ftrokes and dar-
ing metaphors, that aroufed, aftonifhed, and
fhook his hearers to the inmoft foul.   It was the
thunder of oratory, which levelled all oppofition
with a feeming fupernatural power, flafhing conviction on the fenfe, and exciting a mingled tranfport of reverence and terror *.

IN his youth he had exercifed the profeffion of
arms ; and, had he profecuted that employment,
would, in all probability, have rivalled the greateft
commanders of the republic ; for, with the moft
penetrating genius, he poffeffed the moft active
intrepidity.   He was afterwards promoted to the
poft of *Quæflor*, or Paymafter-General to the

* Ἐπεὶ δὲ ὥσπερ ἡ τῶν πλασσομένων καὶ γραφομένων,
Διοσκόρων ὁμοιότης ἔχει τινὰ τᾶ πυκλικᾶ πρὸς τὸν δερμικὸν
ἰσπὶ τῆς μορφῆς διαφοξάν, ἄτω των νεανίσκων ἐκείνων ἐν πολλῇ
τῇ πρὸς ἀνδρείαν καὶ σωφροσυνη, ἔτι δὲ ἐλευθεριότητα καὶ
λογιότητα καὶ μεγαλοψυχίαν ἐμφερείᾳ, μιγάλαι περὶ τὰ
ἔργα καὶ τὰς πολιτείας οἷον ἐξηνθησαν καὶ διεφάνησαν
ἀνομοιότητες· ἃ χεῖρον εἶναί μοι δοκεῖ ταύτας προεκθέσθαι.
πρῶτον μὲν ἂν ἰδίᾳ προσώπῳ καὶ βλέμματι καὶ κινήματί
πρᾷ⊙ καὶ καταστηματικὸς ἦν ὁ Τιβέρι⊙, ἴλιον⊙ δὲ καὶ
σφοδρὸς

forces; an office which had proved a fource of opulence to almoft every perfon by whom it had been enjoyed. This he executed with the moft punctual attention to the neceffities of the foldiery, and fuch difintereſled regard to the ſevereſt dictates of honour, as not only conciliated the warmeſt affection of the troops, but even infpired foreign potentates with admiration and eſteem *.

Courage, moderation, liberality, public ſpirit, and greatneſs of foul, were qualities which the Two Brothers held in common, with a glowing ſenſe of friendſhip, and a philoſophical contempt of pleaſure. Theſe advantages were reinforced by a dignified air, an engaging countenance, and all thoſe graces of nature which could ſerve as a recommendation to ſuch fuperlative merit †.

σφοδρὸς ι Γάϊ☉· ἔπειτα ι Λογ☞ τῷ μεν Γαΐ☉ φοβερὸς καὶ περιπαθὴς εἰς δείνωσιν, ἡδίων δὲ ὁ τῦ Τιβερίυ, καὶ μᾶλλον ἐπαγωγὸς οἴκλυ· τῇ δὲ λιξει καθαρὸς καὶ διαπεπονημέν☉· ἀκριβῶς ἐκεῖν☉, ὁ δὲ Γαΐυ, πιθανὸς καὶ γιγχνωμέν☉. Vide Vertot's Revolution of Rome, lib. viii.

* Καὶ πρῶτον μέν ἐκ Λιβύης παρὰ Μικιψᾶ τῷ βασιλέως πρέσβεις; παραγενομένυς, καὶ λέγονίας ὡς; ὁ βασιλεὺς χάριλι Γαΐυ Γραχχυ πέμψειεν εἰς Σαρδόνα σῖτοι τῷ ςρατηγῷ, δυσχερχόνοιλι; ἐξίβαλον.

† The following Extracts from Dr. Smollett's Dedication of the British Magazine to Mr. Pitt

may

may ferve to complete the PARALLEL, which fome readers may perhaps think, would feem to conclude rather abruptly :

" Malice itfelf muft own, that whatever the warmeft imagination could fuggeft, whatever the fondeft hope could prefage, from your fublime talents and incorruptible integrity, hath been more than realized by your conduct, fince you charged yourfelf with the direction of public affairs.

" Endowed by nature with that vigour of mind which conftitutes the true bafis of magnanimity, and animated with fuch patriot zeal as would have dignified the firft citizen of the Roman republic, you have reftored your country to that rank which fhe ought to maintain among the nations. You have healed her divifions, abolifhed the diftinctions of party, and, by your own perfonal importance, united all your fellow fubjects in one generous and hearty concurrence to fupport the dignity and profecute the true intereft of the Common-wealth.

" You have infpired our councils with courage, fortitude, and wifdom : you have directed our national efforts to the purfuit of true glory and infallible fuccefs. Under the aufpices of your Miniftry, diftinguifhed above all others for vigilance, fteadinefs, and forefight, our arms by fea and land are again accuftomed to triumph : they have raifed immortal trophies in the four divifions of the globe. Europe, Afia, Africa, and America, have in their turns beheld illuftrious proofs of Britifh valour ; and Victory feems to have chofen her ftation between the knees of our aged Sovereign.

" Embellifhed with thefe great and glorious events, this period will, in the annals of Great Britain, fhine with unrivalled and unfading luftre. The adminiftration of a PITT, fo dear to the prefent age, which fills our mouths with praife and our hearts with exultation, will become the hiftorian's favourite æra, and prove, to lateft pofterity, a darling theme of admiration and applaufe."

E S S A Y   II.

OMRAH, the fon of Abulfaid, of the feed
of the faithful, native of the city of Bir,
in the province of Diarbekr, or Algiezirah, ferti-
lized by the waters of El-pharat *, being fired by
the pride of youth, and ftimulated by a thirft after
knowledge, refolved to improve his mind by travelling into foreign countries. He accordingly
mounted his camel, and departed with the caravan
for Bafrah, where he arrived without accident,
and made a confiderable purchafe of the moft
beautiful pearls. Having thus far happily performed
his journey, his heart panted with defire to vifit
the imperial city of Baghdad, where he might be
an eye-witnefs of the glory and magnificence that
furrounded the perfon of the renowned khaliph
Haroun al Rafchid, the fublime fucceffor of the
Prophet, the emperor of the faithful, the rofe of
delight, the fteward of Paradife, the cherifher
of merit, whofe countenance fhone like the vifion

* The Euphrates is called by the natives El-pharat.

B 4   of

of Al Borak *, whofe wings were perpetually drop-
ping with the dews of liberality, and extended for
fhelter to all the children of diftrefs.

OMRAH, elevated with fuccefs, and glowing
with the reflection of his own importance, confidered through the medium of youthful vanity,
fet out from Bafrah, without guide or company,
and had already advanced as far as the delightful
plains of Hella, within a day's journey of the
great city. The fun had begun to gild the horizon; the heavens difplayed an unclouded ex-
panfe of blue ferenity ; the fig-tree, the citron,
the palm, and pomegranate, feemed to open their
arms to welcome the new-born day; the verdant
plants that adorn the banks of El-pharat, glittered with the dew-drops of the morning ; the
young camel, the wanton fawn, the bounding
antelope, and nimble zebra, fported along the
meads, and every bufh refounded with the melody of the winged chorifters. Every thing concurred to fill the heart of our youth with gaiety
and good-humour, and infpire his breaft with
that felf-confidence which never fails to darken
the natural lights of fenfe and reafon. Here he

* Al Borak, according to the Koran, was the beaft that
carried Mahomet to heaven. His face was like that of a man ;
and his eyes fhone with as great a luftre as the ftars would difplay, were they enlightened by the rays of the fun.

                                              was

was overtaken by two perfonages, whofe appearance forthwith attracted his attention. One of
them feemed to be a man in ftature, but a child in
countenance : his eyes were vacant, his features
inanimated ; his mouth was unfurnifhed with
teeth, and an infipid fmile languifhed inceffantly on
his face. His neck was hung round with tinkling
cymbals : in his hand he carried a pole, to the end
of which was fixed the bladder of a dromedary,
diftended with air, and containing a few polifhed
pebbles. This inftrument he rattled ever and anon,
and feemed to take pleafure in the found it produced. His companion, who performed the office of tutor, and led him by a bow-ftring faf-
tened to his girdle, appeared to be of the middle
age, tall, robuft, and brawny, with a brindled
beard and froward vifage. The place of one eye
was covered with a patch of black taffeta; the
other, furrounded with a livid circle, glared like
a comet portending the vengeance of heaven : his
nofe,which was curved like the ftaff of the khaliph,
had been levelled to his face by the ftroke of accident ; his forehead was indented with fcars ; his
teeth were broken and difplaced ; his turban was
ftained with blood : his garment was torn, and he
halted on one leg like Ebn Zaid, the emir of
Moufful. A fcymetar of Damafcus hung upon
his thigh, without a fcabbard ; and in his hand he
bore a fplintered lance, the remains of fome tour-

B 5   nament

nament in which he had been engaged. Notwithftanding his ferocious appearance, he accofted our
traveller in a courteous manner; and, underftanding his purpofe of vifiting Baghdad, offered to
conduct him the neareft way to that city. Omrah being naturally affable, accepted this offer,
and, joining thefe two ftrangers, was agreeably entertained with the fingular adventures which the
lame tutor recounted.

At length they arrived at the foot of a mountain, where the road was divided into two paths :
one of thefe was wide, fafe, and agreeable, wind-
ing along the level plain, fo as to form a confiderable circuit ; the other, dangerous and difficult,
afcended the mountain, and, in one place; bordered on the brink of a precipice that overhung
the river El-pharat, at that time fwelled by the
vernal rains. This, as the fhorteft, was chofen
by the lame guide ; and Omrah followed his footfteps, even againft the dictates of his own judgement; but he was overawed by the fear of appearing
pufillanimous in the fight of his conductor. They
had made confiderable progrefs, notwithftanding
the inconveniencies of the way, when, in paffing
over the edge of a fteep rock, the younger of his
two fellow-travellers fhook his rattle ; the noife
of which alarmed an owl, that repofed herfelf in
a fmall thicket which bordered on the path. Af-
frighted

frighted at the found, fhe flapped her wings, and
fcreeching at the fame time, darted full in the face
of the aftonifhed Omrah, who, ftarting with furprife, fell over the precipice, and plunged into
the waves of the El-pharat. Though he had the
reputation of an excellent fwimmer, fuch was
the rapidity of the ftream as to hurry him more
than ten parafangs below the place where he fell :
but at length he reached the fhore, half dead with
terror, fatigue, and vexation : for he had loft his
turban, which was adorned with jewels of ineftimable value. In this deplorable fituation he was
found by a peafant, who conveyed him to his cottage, and adminiftered to him with great humanity in the courfe of a fever, which the agitation
of his mind and body had produced.

ONE day while he wandered among the groves of
citrons that fkirted the river, to inhale the refrefh-
ing air, and congratulated himfelf upon his recovery, his eyes were fuddenly dazzled with the ap-
parition of a female, fo ravifhingly beautiful, that
he miftook her for one of the Houri, thofe immortal daughters of delight, with whom the faithful
Moflems folace themfelves in Paradife. Her eyes
were black, large, and comely, like thofe of the
wanton heifer that crops the yellow flowers in the
enamelled meadows of Yerak : her cheeks glowed
with the crimfon dye of youth, more gorgeous

B 6

than

than the full blown rofe that perfumes the gardens
of Damafcus : her teeth were white, and polifhed
as the fceptre of the khaliph, and regularly fet,
like the rows of cyprefs that fhade the bazars of
Diarbekr : her raven treffes, that flowed adown
her fhoulders, were interwoven with fprigs of dia-
monds, which fparkled like the ftars of heaven
through the fable curtain of the night : her neck
was fnowy as the flour of Ophra, elegantly
turned, fmooth, and gloffy, like the fwans that
ride upon the waters of Diglut * : her breafts were
feen to rife through a tranfparent veil, like two
marble cupolas in the ftately mofque of Bir. In
a word, her form was exquifite, and her fplendid
apparel fo contrived as to exhibit every charm to the
greateft advantage. She turned her eyes upon
Omrah, and her look was accompanied with fuch
a fmile as captivated the fenfe, and kindled in his
heart a tranfport of defire. When fhe retired,
he followed her fteps to the purlieus of her habitation, which might be juftly termed the Bower
of Blifs, fo lavifhly was it adorned with all the
beauties of nature and of art. Here he was
checked by reverential awe, afraid of intruding
upon the privacy of fome voluptuous Genie, who
he fuppofed had fixed her refidence in this enchanting fpot.

* The River Tigris, fo called.

WHILE

WHILE he ftood hefitating between love and apprehenfion, he was joined by an impetuous youth, with ruddy locks and grey eyes, that glanced like the pearls of Bafrah : his nofe was aquiline, and his complexion fo florid, that his blood feemed ready to burft the veffels in which it was contained. His breath was more fcorching than the blaft called *famiel*, that fmites the traveller even to the marrow ; and his fkin felt like the touch of the angel of fire : his robe was ftained with the juice of the grape, forbid to the followers of the Prophet : he fmelled like the rams of Khurdiftan ; and brandifhed a dagger, that glittered like the *fam famah* of the invincible Haroun al Rafchid. He approached Omrah without fpeaking, and, feizing his hand, conveyed him with the fwiftnefs of lightning to the bower of the beautiful unknown. There he met with fuch reception as fuited his moft fanguine wifh : the enchantrefs flew to his embrace, and he took full poffeffion of her charms ; fo that for fome time his fenfes were drowned in extafy.

BUT alas! this tranfport was of fhort duration : next morning waking from his trance, he found himfelf ftretched among ftraw in a wretched folitary hut, abandoned by his inamorata, and robbed of all his pearls. He ftarted up with horror, and, rufhing into the open air, perceived that all the gaiety of the landfcape

landfcape was vanifhed. Cafting his eyes around, he
beheld nothing but a dreary wafte of brakes and
bogs, roughened with fome rugged rocks, among
which he faw fome half-ftarved goats and mon-
kies, the emblems of lewdnefs and obfcenity. At
length in a dark corner of the cottage he difcovered an old hag, lying extended on a mat, and
groaning with all the agony of diftemper. He approached this miferable object, notwithftanding
an almoft intolerable ftench that annoyed his noftrils ; but fhe was incapable of conveying the leaft
verbal information. There was hardly any vef-
tige of her nofe remaining : her teeth, her palate,
and her throat, were half confumed with putrefy-
ing fores. What he could not learn from her
tongue, he guefled from her condition. Dread
and abhorrence winged his flight from this infec-
tious fcene. Smiting his breaft in a tranfport of
confternation and remorfe, " O Allah ! (cried he)
is this the fruit of that virtuous education which
I imbibed at Bir under the wings of my indul-
gent parents ! Are thefe the effects of the fage
precepts inculcated on my tender mind by the
venerable Abulfaid, whofe wifdom diffufed a grateful odour, like the gums and fpices of Yeman ?
Wretched Omrah ! how have thy folly and mifconduct difgraced thy family, and brought thee
to fhame and perdition ? Thou haft obeyed the
impulfe of the moft brutal and dangerous paffions!

                                        Thou

Thou haſt ruſhed into the arms of vice, and held
guilty dalliance with infamy and difeafe ?   Thou
art ſtripped of all thy wealth, derived from inhe-
ritance and induſtry : thy morals are corrupted,
and in thy fleſh are fown the feeds of pain and pu-
trefaction ! Die, miferable Omrah ! for thou art
unworthy to live, or be numbered among the followers of the Prophet.'' So faying, he pulled
from his girdle a poignard which his evil fortune
had fpared, and, calling upon the angel of the dead,
would have buried it in his bofom, had not
his hand been fuddenly arreſted.   Thus reſtrained,
he turned about, and found himfelf withheld by
an aged Dervife, whofe appearance infpired him
with reverence and awe.   His eyes were bright
and piercing, like thofe of the eagle of Irak ; but
his looks were mild and benign : every feature
breathed fenfibility ;   and the difpofition of the
whole formed an amiable afpect of fweetnefs and
compofure.   Age had robbed his forehead of its
honours ; but his white beard defcended to his
middle.   He was cloathed in a fimple garment of
camel's hair ; his feet were defended by fandals cf
packthread ; and in his hand he held a rofary,
according to the cuſtom of the Moſlem devotees.

HAVING recited the apothegm of Allah Ack-
bar, God is good, " Hold, my fon (faid he), nor
meanly give way to the frantic dictates of defpair :
remember

remember what thou oweft to thyfelf, thy family, thy country, and thy religion. Confider, the life which thou art rafhly going to throw away is not at thy difpofal; it is a facred truft, for which thou art accountable to the great Giver. He it is that placed thee in this fublunary ftate of pro-bation, to fulfil the wife purpofes of Providence; and fhalt thou revolt againft his decrees, and, like a coward or a traitor, abandon thy poft with-out permiflion? Wilt thou rufh precipitately into the prefence of the offended Allah? Wilt thou prefume to mingle with the pure fpirits of the faith-ful, ftained as thou muft be with the dreadful guilt of fuicide? Thy country demands that life which thou haft no right to take away. In with-drawing thyfelf from the land of the living, thou robbeft thy Prince of a fubject; thou robbeft the community of thofe talents which were beftowed upon thee for the ufe and benefit of thy fellow-ci-tizens; and thou entaileft difgrace upon the family which gave thee being. Wilt thou then plunge into eternity, with fuch complicated horrors on thy head? Ah! no. Let it not be faid, that the feed of a believing Muffulman, trained up in the true faith of the ever-bleffed Prophet, and admit-ted to kifs the facred threfhold of the Caabah, fhould bring forth fuch bitter fruit of wickednefs and woe."

EVERY

EVERY word which the fenior fpoke, feemed to penetrate to the heart of Omrah; the poignard dropped from his hand; the agitation of his mind fubfided; his looks foftened into the expreffion of penitential forrow; and his cheeks were bedewed with the tears of contrition. He fell on his knees before the reverend Dervife, and grafping his hand, " Father (cried he), I fubmit to the irrefiftible force of your reafon. You have taught me to acquiefce in the difpenfations of Providence : pity an haplefs young man, far removed from the advice and affiftance of his friends, mifled by the paffions of youth, perfecuted by misfortune, and betrayed by iniquity. You have faved me from the commiffion of a crime, the remembrance of which fills me with horror. Extend your charity ftill farther, and aid me with your falutary counfel, more precious than the fragrant gums of Hayaman ; counfel flowing from the facred fprings of ftudy and experience."

AFTER this preamble, he recounted the difafters which had befallen him, and defcribed the fnares into which he had fallen. The Dervife, having liftened to his tale with the moft humane complacency, undertook the office of comforter, bade him be of good cheer, and thank heaven for the dangers he had efcaped. He obferved, that adverfity was the moft ufeful fchool of life : he demonftrated the

infig-

infignificance and fugitive nature of wealth : he
reminded him of his youth, vigour and qualifications, and unfolded a variety of fair profpects for
the exertion of his induftry and perfeverance ; he
promifed to fecure his conftitution by means of an
antidote, the juice of a certain herb which grows
upon the mountains of Kurdo, lately difcovered by
the khaliph's phyfician Gabriel, the fon of Bakhtifou, an heretic of the fuperftition of the Jefides :
finally, he invited him to his hermitage in the
neighbourhood, whither he was accompanied by
the grateful Omrah.

EVERY word that flowed from the mouth of
the Dervife was pointed with wifdom, or fmoothed
with humanity.   His converfation ftole imper-
ceptibly into the heart of Omrah, and his de-
meanour infpired him with reverence and affection.   He was commodioufly lodged in the hermitage, and treated with parental care, unde-
bauched by vitious tendernefs ; for he found himfelf reftricted to the food of temperance and fruga-
lity, while his hoft adminiftered to him the promifed antidote, which in a little time deftroyed the
feeds of that poifon which had begun to germinate
in his conftitution.   It was a much more difficult
tafk to purify his mind, and eradicate thofe bad habits which youth and paffion had engendered : this,
however, the Dervife did not decline, as he perceived

ceived in his pupil a remarkable fenfibility of heart, together with an uncommon acutenefs and ductility of underftanding. His vanity and pride were already mortified by the difafters he had un-dergone : but that mortification was the effect of difappointment ; and thofe paffions would, in all probability, have revived in proportion as the fenfe of calamity abated, if the Dervife had not taken a more effectual method to fubdue them with the arms of reafon and philofophy. He made a fair eftimate of all the young man's accomplifh-ments, balanced them with his defects, and fhewed how the latter fcale preponderated. He proved, that, in point of perfonal qualification, he was equalled, if not excelled, by many of his cotemporaries: that he was rivalled in beauty by the phyfician Gabriel, the fon of Bakhtifou : that he could not throw the javelin like Mufa Ebn Ifa, the præfect of Egypt ; nor manage the fteed like Moflema Ebn Yahya, who had been trained up with the khaliph ; nor run the tilt like Amru Ebn Mahran, who won the prize in the famous tourna-ment held at Gezirah, built on an Ifland of Diglut. He obferved, that Omrah could not be more loyal than Yahya Ebn Khalid Ebn Baramack ; nor more liberal than his fon Giafar, the firft favourite of the empire, on whom the khaliph beftowed his own fifter in marriage ; nor more brave than this

favourite's

favourite's brother, Fadl, who extinguifhed the rebellion of Yahya Ebn Abdallah. Such were the qualities of the celebrated houfe of Baramack. He convinced him, that in point of genius and knowledge, he could not be compared to many of the khaliph's flaves : that in poetry he was infinitely furpaffed by Abounaovas, who compofed the famous ftanza upon the verfe fent by one of the Queen's damfels to Haroun al Rafchid : that in piety he fell far fhort of Ebn Adhem, who, in a vifion, faw the angel writing his name among thofe who fincerely loved their Creator : that in medicine he was ignorant, in comparifon of the Chriftian Gabriel and the Indian Manghch ; which laft was faid to have the hand of Mofes and the breath of Meffiah : that in metaphyfics he was eclipfed by Aboufaid Afami, who wrote the famous treatife on the fublime doƈrines of the foul, intituled, Fahouat-u al naderat ; and that he was a child in philofophy and jurifprudence, when compared to Morabek and Bahaloul. Finally, he reminded our youth of the diftrefsful circumftances to which he was reduced by the lofs of his turban, and the treachery of her with whom he had held vicious dalliance.

By thefe and other fuch wife remonftrances, the difpofition of Omrah was entirely changed. He began to look upon himfelf with that contempt and diffidence,

fidence, which lay the foundations of wisdom. His heart, which pride had hardened, was now melted by humanity, and overflowed with all the tendernefs of benevolence : all the vain projects of his early youth vanished, like the phantoms of a morning dream : he obtained an abfolute victory over his moft unruly paffions ; and now retained no ambition but that of diftinguifhing himfelf among his fellow-creatures by his fuperior fagacity and virtue. In thefe fentiments, he liftened with the moft eager attention to the inftructions of the Dervife, who was not only confummate mafter of all the philofophy and learning of the Eaft, but likewife fkilled in the policy of nations, the cuftoms and manners of mankind, and intimately acquainted with all the fprings that move the human mind. His knowledge was fo univerfal, and his virtue fo fublime, that Omrah believed him a fupernatural being, and could hardly refrain from worfhip and adoration. He did not fail, however, to make advantage of the precious moments which the opportunity offered. He carefully treafured up the leffons of his tutor, and, in one annual revolution of the fun, his mind was fo well ftored with wifdom and erudition, that the Dervife pronounced him qualified as a profeffor in the famous college at Madrafah al Moftan Seriah, which the khaliph had lately eftablifhed in the city of Baghdad.

dad. Neverthelefs, Omrah was not yet fatisfied
with the proficiency he had made, and refolved to
pafs another year in the profecution of his ftudies,
within the bofom of this charming retreat, when
his refolution was fruftrated by an unexpected
event. From the aga of the caravan of Bir, which
paffed near the fkir's of the hermitage, he learned
that the venerable Abulfaid had paid his debt to
nature; and that his mother, the virtuous Kadifha,
mourned, without ceafing, the death of her hufband, and the abfence of her fon, of whom fhe
had heard no tidings fince his departure.

OMRAH's filial tendernefs was waked by this
intelligence. Having paid the tribute of tears to
the memory of his father, he confulted the Dervife
with refpect to his future conduct, and was ex-
horted to return to Bir, and fettle the affairs of
his family. Being enriched with other falutary
advice, he took leave of his kind preceptor, joined
the caravan, arrived at Bir, comforted his mother,
and found himfelf heir to a confiderable fortune.
Mindful of the Dervife's injunctions, he converted
his eftate into jewels, and fet out the neareft road
for Baghdad, determined to devote his talents to
the fervice of his country. He again departed
with the caravan for Moufful, which was chiefly
loaded with dyed goat-fkins, linen and cotton ;
                                            and

and on the plains of Orfa had an opportunity of fignalizing his valour in an engagement with a body of Curdes and Tartars, who attacked the efcorte, and were routed after a fevere action, in which Omrah flew with his own hand one of the fierceft Scheicks of the enemy. They paffed over the verdant hills of Hojalor, covered with fheep, and through the vales of Murdin, fhaded with the date, the fig, and the pomegranate :- then making a circuit round the mountains of Balad, they vifited the ancient city of Nifibin, watered by the delightful ftream of Hermas. Having croffed the ftately bridge of Nifibin, they for five days travelled through the parched and defart country of Sinjar, before they reached the fpacious city of Moufful, feated on the pleafant banks of the Diglut.

EVEN the delicious melons which this territory affords, and the curiofities with which the place abounds, could not, in the opinion of Omrah, make atonement for the exceffive heat that reigns here in the fummer : he therefore quitted it with the firft opportunity, and profecuting his journey by the way of Karkak, arrived in fafety at the Imperial city of Baghdad, the centre of terreftrial paradife, and the pearl of human greatnefs.

IT was in the night al Kadr, denominated of divine decree, in the month Ramadan, that Omrah

rah entered the weſtern city, called Kafr, and was
ſtruck dumb with aſtoniſhment and admiration at
ſight of the Dar al Khali'a, or palace of the immortal Haroun al Raſchid, who ſat inthroned
above the Princes of the nations, in a blaze of
ſplendor that dazzled the eyes, and confounded
the pride, of all beholders.

OMRAH proſtrated himſelf in a tranſport of
wonder and delight, and found himſelf irreſiſtibly
attracted by an eager deſire to be received among
the ſervants of the invincible khaliph. He ſpent
the firſt days after his arrival in ſurveying the
moſques, the bazars, the palaces, gardens, and
canals of this magnificent city : then he conſulted
the khaliph's jeweller, to whom he had been recommended by one of his kinſmen at Bir.

THIS perſon, whoſe name was Ali Ebn Azrah,
conducted him to a field on the farther ſide of the
Diglut ; where he perceived, on the ſummit of a
very high mountain, ſeemingly inacceſſible, a
temple that ſhone like adamant. " Behold, ſaid
Ali, the hill of Akoba, and *Caſtle of Diſtinction*,
which every man muſt reach before he can obtain
the favour of the khaliph. The attempt is attended with imminent danger ; and incredible labour, as well as ſkill, muſt be exerted by him who
climbs the precipice, treads the burning ſands,

paſſes

paſſes through the almoſt impenetrable brake, and diſcomfits the formidable guards that hover about the ſkirts of the fortreſs."

THE peril and difficulties annexed to this enterprize, ſerved only to inflame the ambition of Omrah, who would have begun the aſcent without heſitation, had he not been aſſured by Ali, that each adventurer was permitted to chuſe two guides from a multitude of perſonages who conſtantly plied at the foot of the hill, on purpoſe to be employed. Of theſe he ſelected the firſt that engaged his attention. This was a florid youth, with an inſinuating look and ever-dimpling ſmile, that played upon his viſage like the circling eddies that ſportive whirl upon the tranſparent ſtream of Belikah. He was tall, ſtraight, and vigorous; ſtrong as the Camel of Halab, and nimble as al Jerbua of the deſert. His robe was covered with the moſt luxuriant deſigns of embroidery: in his left hand he held a vial, caſed in filigrane of gold; and in his right a picture of the caſtle, drawn with ſuch exquiſite art as to faſcinate the eyes of the ſpectator. This he no ſooner preſented to the view of Omrah, than our youth was ſeized with an extaſy of impatience to atchieve the adventure ; for the painter had not only repreſented all the beauties and elegancies of the temple with the moſt

VOL. I. C flattering

/

flattering exaggeration, but alfo exhibited Hazima, the caliph's treafurer, fitting on a throne
before the portal, diftributing, with a liberal hand,
preferment, honours, and rewards, to the happy
few who reached the area of the caftle. The
other guide whom Omrah chofe, formed a remarkable contraft with the former. He feemed
to be turned of fifty, thick, fquat, and broad-
fhouldered; cloathed in a plain garment, girded
about his loins with ropes called *ypes*, ufed by the
porters of Baghdad. His features were contracted
not fo much by age as by a continued feverity of
attention; and his eyes gleamed from under his
wrinkled forehead, like two unpolifhed carbuncles
fhining through the rugged cliffs of Araban. He
examined our youth with the moft minute and curious furvey; then buckled on his head a helmet
of cork, and taking in his hand a long pole, with
an iron hook at one end, walked with a firm and
deliberate pace behind Omrah, who eagerly followed the footfteps of his youthful conductor. He
was already almoft fainting with fatigue when he
had furmounted one precipice, and faw another
above him much more high, and almoft perpen-
dicular. His heart began to fail at this profpect,
when the junior held up the picture before his eyes,
and at the fame time prefented the vial, exhorting
him to fwallow a mouthful of that incomparable
cordial.

cordial. He complied with this advice, and found
it more delicious than the fherbet of Ophra, com-
pounded for the haram of the khaliph. His fpirits
were not only inftantaneoufly refrefhed, but his
heart was infpired with fuch confidence as he had
never felt before, and his looks were lighted up
with a tranfport of courage and ambition. The
triumvirate now ftood upon the projection of a
rock about fix feet fquare ; and the younger of his
guides, having pocketed his picture and vial, began
to climb the fteep rock, which in fome meafure
over-hung this refting-place. He had already
fixed his right hand on the brink of the fummit,
when the fenior fuddenly feizing Omrah, threw
him flat on the ground in an inftant, and, extending himfelf upon his body, preffed him to the rock
with irrefiftible force.

OUR adventurer had not time to expoftulate on
this feeming outrage. The firft object he perceived was his youthful conductor tumbling down
from the fummit, in fuch a direction, that, if the
fenior had not committed this violence, he muft
have ftruck him in his fall, and dafhed him in
pieces among the rocks which they had already afcended.

THE part of the fummit on which the guide had
laid hold was a loofe fragment, that feparated from

the

the rock, and pitched upon the helmet of the elder guide, from whence it rebounded harmlefs,
and fell at a confiderable diftance from the foot of
the precipice.

OMRAH, in the midft of his acknowledgments
to his fage preferver, could not help lamenting the
lofs of his other attendant, when the old man bade
him caft his eyes below, where he faw him limp-
ing off the field, in all appearance very little da-
maged by his fall, though he did not attempt to
re-afcend the rock to the affiftance of his pupil.

THE remaining guide, having obferved the precipice above with great attention, unbound his
ypes; one end of which he tied round the middle
of Omrah, keeping the other faft about his own
body; then fixing the hook of his pole upon the
trunk of a wild afh, which grew from a cleft in
the rock, he drew himfelf up, and afterwards, by
means of the rope, dragged Omrah into the fame
hollow. This operation being repeated, they
both reached the fummit in fafety; and our adventurer looked back upon the dangers he had undergone with a mingled tranfport of joy and horror.
Nor was the profpect before him much more com-
fortable. He found himfelf obliged to pafs over a
long tract of loofe burning fand, like that of the
defert of Barkha; at the farther end of which he
                                      perceived

perceived a thick and feemingly impaffable brake of thorns, briars, and brambles; but he faw neither grove nor caravanfera for refrefhment or repofe, nor the leaft fign of water to quench his thirft, which was already become almoft intolerable. He would now have defifted from his purfuit, but there was an impoffibility of retreating, and his guide told him, that his fafety and fuccefs depended entirely upon his perfeverance. He refolved, therefore, to redouble all his efforts; and his companion accommodating him with an occafional umbrella made of the palmetto-leaf, fixed to the end of his pole, he proceeded through the blafted plain with aftonifhing vigour: but when at length he approached the brake, weary, faint, and exhaufted; when he faw how thick the thorns were fet, and how the briars and brambles were entangled together; when he viewed the numerous and dreadful adverfaries whom he had to encounter, on the fpace between this boundary and the drawbridge; he was abandoned by his conftancy and courage; his heart died within him; and he declared he would lie down and perifh among the fcorching fand, rather than encounter fuch infurmountable toils, or engage with fuch an hoft of terrors. His attendant, feeing him overwhelmed with defpair, fought not to animate him to new endeavours. His province was not to ftimulate and

encourage,

encourage, but to forefee danger and prevent ac-- cident. He lifted the youth upon his back, with as much eafe as if he had been a child new born ; and carrying him to the left, about the length of one parafang, arrived at the brink of a rapid ftream, which Omrah beheld with a tranfport of joy: but this was inftantly damped, when he heard his con- ductor exclaim, " Thefe be the waters of Difap- " pointment, too bitter to regale thy palate ; " though, perhaps they may ferve to extinguifh " thy ambition." So faying, he clafped the youth in his arms, and plunged into the torrent, which was equally deep and impetuous.

THE force with which Omrah was precipitated from the bank of the river, funk them both to the bottom, where the fenior difappeared, after having, by a kind of magical conveyance, fixed the hel- met of cork upon the head of his pupil. Thus buoyed, the youth foon rofe to the furface, when he found himfelf dafhed to and fro among various rocks and contending currents ; and in fpite of all his endeavours to the contrary, was obliged to fwallow large draughts of the water, which was ten times more unpalatable than the afhes of the kali, or the falt of Ammon, cryftallized from the urine of Hegen among the fcorching fand of the defart. All his efforts to reach the fhore would have

have been ineffectual, had he not been accommodated with the helmet, which not only defended
his head from violence, but rendered his body fpe-
cifically lighter than the fluid in which he floated.
When his ftrength failed, he recommended his
foul to Allah and the prophet, and refigned himfelf to the violence of the ftream, which tilting
him over a cafcade, loft all its fury in a fpreading
pool below. Here he recollected his thoughts,
and by a fmall exertion of his ftrength and fkill in
fwimming, arrived at the dry land. Neverthelefs
he was fo much exhaufted by the fatigue and terror he had undergone, that he fwooned upon the
bank; and when he recovered the ufe of his fenfes,
found himfelf in a very dangerous fituation.- He
was furrounded by a body of armed Curdes on
horfeback. A lance was held to his throat by a
female warrior, who ftood over him in the attitude of ftriking, holding in her left hand his fcarf
and fcymetar, which fhe had unbound from his
fide; and one of her attendants had taken poffeffion of his helmet.

WHEN he looked up and faw this Amazon, he
thought it was a vifion of the brain, with which
he refolved to regale his fancy. On the crown of
her head arofe the Botta, adorned with jewels like
the tiara of Irak; and her long black hair, tied

C 4   together

together with a filken fillet, flowed down in natural ringlets to the middle of her back, floating
and fluctuating on the wanton wind. Her fhoulder was graced with an emboffed quiver, plentifully fupplied with arrows ; and on the fame fide
was flung a bow tipped with ivory, and ftudded
with precious ftones. Her upper garment was
faced with ermin, wide, fhort, and open, difplaying the under ftole of rich Perfian, bound about
her middle with a fcarf of Damafcus, but parting
at the knee fo as to difclofe her delicate limbs cafed
in embroidered bufkins. Her face was beautiful
as the idea that true Moflems have of the Carubun
and Sajeduh, angels that adore the Moft High in
the feventh heaven ; and her eyes lightened like
the precious ftone of Hafala, which the prophet
faw in the vifion Borak. Though her pofture was
menacing, her looks were benign ; and through
the refentment that glowed on her vifage, there
fhone fuch an emanation of foftnefs and complacency, that the firft emotion of Omrah was not
fear, but admiration and love. '' Haplefs wretch !
(cried fhe in a tone fweet as the murmurs of al
Cawthur, the fountains that warble as they flow
from under the tree Sedrut) recommend thyfelf to
the faithful of God, the angel of death that pre-
fides over feventy thoufand, who is now ready to
blot thy detefted name from the book of life.—
                           Thou

Thou haſt ſlain the young prince of the Curdes, my betrothed lord ; theſe be the trophies of thy cruel victory. This ſcarf I wove with my own fingers, ſitting in my bower, by one of the ſprings of Amada on the mountain." "Fair princeſs (replied the youth), cruelty and injuſtice cannot lurk under ſuch an aſpect of innocence and humanity. My heart is more endangered by the ſhafts of your beauty, than by the point of your lance. The ſcarf you have recognized was fairly won in battle, from a perſon who attacked me without provocation. Nevertheleſs, if it has been my misfortune unwillingly to incur the diſpleaſure of ſuch perfection, execute your threats. I will gladly die by your avenging hand ; but I cannot live the object of your reſentment."

AT theſe words her cheeks were overſpread with a deep ſuffuſion ; ſhe withdrew her lance, ſaying, " I will not ſtain myſelf with thy blood ; thou ſhalt be reſerved for the juſtice of my ſovereign, whoſe camp is pitched in the receſs of a deep valley to the northward of yonder ſhaggy mountain." He was accordingly fettered by her retinue, and mounted behind one of the horſemen, with whom ſhe forthwith ſet out on her return from the excurſion ſhe had made. They were benighted in a thick wood, where they pitched occaſional tents,

in one of which Omrah was fecured under a ftrong
guard. At midnight, while he ruminated on his
hard fate, his lovely enflaver on a fudden ftood
before him, her eyes ftreaming with tears.
"Stranger (cried fhe), this is no time for diffem-
bling ; thou haft made an impreffion on my heart.
Far from dragging thee before the footftool of Amru, who would devote thee to inftant death for the
murder of his fon, I will inftantly fet thee free,
and am almoft tempted to follow thy fortune.
Here, take thy fcymetar, and wear the fcarf for
my fake ! Thou art more worthy than its former
poffeffor, the moft brutal of all the Scheicks in
Curdiftan. Two horfemen, whom I have felected
for the purpofe, wait without to conduct thee beyond the fartheft extent of our hoftile inroads upon
Yeman.   Arife without delay, and profit by this
precious opportunity ; which if once loft, will
never be retrieved."   Omrah's whole foul was
diffolved in tendernefs by this unexpected adddrefs.
He proftrated himfelf before her, and declared in
the moft paffionate ftrain, that he fhould have
more joy in dying at her feet, than in tafting the
greateft favours that fortune could beftow without her prefence and participation. "You muft
not die (fhe haftily exclaimed) : fuch an event
would prove fatal to her whom you pretend to
love. Know, that although I live among thefe
                                         barbarous

barbarous tribes, I am not by birth a Curde : recommend me to thy Prophet, whom 1 alſo adore :
away, and remember the unfortunate Fatima." So
ſaying, ſhe made a ſignal, in conſequence of which
the two horſemen entered the tent, ſeized our
youth by the arms, and conveying him to the
door, lifted him up on a beautiful ſteed gaily capa-
riſoned.   They mounted their horſes at the ſame
time, and one of them taking hold of the reins of
his bridle, they proceeded in ſilence, the heart of
Omrah being overwhelmed with grief, anxiety,
and confuſion.

AFTER having traverſed ſeveral thickets,
marſhes, and mountains, they found themſelves in the morning on the ſkirts of an ex-
tenſive plain ; when one of the two conductors
quitting the bridle of Omrah's horſe, pointed with
his finger to the Eaſt ; and the youth, caſting his
eyes that way, diſcerned the towers and minarets
of Baghdad : then the Curdes, laying the finger
to the lip, as a ſignal to enjoin ſilence, turned about
their horſes, and rode off at full ſpeed, leaving the
ſon of Abulfaid to proſecute his reflections on the
ſtrange viciſſitudes of his fortune. It was not without the utmoſt perplexity that he revolved a variety
of thoughts, in which the amiable Fatima ſtill
maintained the aſcendancy ſhe had ſo ſurpriſingly

C 6   acquired.

acquired. Her beauteous image was ftill prefent
to his fancy, and her laft words ftill founded in his
tars : " Remember the unfortunate Fatima !"
Sometimes he was tempted to return and regale
himfelf with another fight of her, though at the
certain expence of his life. Sometimes he was
tired with the hope of giving fuch information to
the khaliph, as would induce him to fend a body
of troops to intercept the Curdes in their retreat :
the firft, upon recollection, appeared to be a fcheme
fuggefted by madnefs; the other he forefaw would
be impracticable. At length he refolved to retire
from the hurry of courts and cities, and cultivate
the virtues of private life in fome quiet retreat.
The very fpot over which he now travelled, feemed
remarkably adapted by nature for the fcene of his
retirement. It was a delightful plain, waved into
a number of agreeable fwells, tufted with groves,
and watered with tranfparent ftreamlets. Befides,
it could not be far diftant from the recefs haunted
by the Curdes, among whom his Fatima refided ;
and he was flattered with the hope of one day re-
viewing the idol of his foul. Stimulated by thefe
confiderations, he withdrew his effects from the
hands of the jeweller Ali Ebn Azrah ; agreed
with the Emir of the province about the purchafe
of the land upon which he had pitched for a fettle-
ment; reared up an houfe with furprifing expedition;

ftocked

ftocked his ground with cattle of all forts ; bought
a number of flaves, and parcelled out the ground
into corn fields, paftures, and plantations. Providence crowned his endeavours with fuccefs. Yellow harvefts waved on every fide : his flocks and
herds multiplied with amazing increafe : his gardens and orchards glowed with the moft delicious
fruits ; the citron, the melon, the pomegranate,
the peach, and the nectarine. His fleeces rivalled
the fineft wool of Curdiftan : and, even before
the firft year of his rufticity was elapfed, he fent
a large quantity of raw filks and camels hair to the
bazars of Baghdad. His extenfive œconomy required a great many hands, and fed a confiderable
number of dependants: his herdfmen, peafants,
and flaves, partook and rejoiced in his good fortune. All his fellow-creatures were welcome to ,
his advice and affiftance ; and his hand was ever
ready to relieve the neceffitous. In a word, his
name was diffufed like a Sabæan odour, and every
hill and valley refounded with ftrains that were
poured forth in praife of Omrah, whom they compared to the patriarch Al Ma'mur, father of the
faithful.

In the midft of all thefe enjoyments, which
muft have been exquifitely felt by a perfon
of Omrah's generous difpofition, he ftill retained
                                                    the

the idea of the fair Fatima, though it no longer
excited painful fenfations, but rather a tender remembrance, which he cherifhed with a kind of
melancholy felf-indulgence. Two years had happily rolled over his head in this pacific ftate of rural fequeftration, when one evening, ftanding in
his porch to enjoy the cooling breeze, he lifted up
his eyes, and beheld his friend the Dervife ad-
vancing towards his habitation. He ran forth to
meet his worthy preceptor, and, falling on his
neck, wept aloud in a tranfport of joy. Then
he led him by the hand into his Divan, and wel-
comed his arrival with fuch overflowing of gratitude, as might be expected from the benevolent
heart of Omrah. When the fage had refrefhed
and repofed himfelf, his kind hoft recounted all
the particulars of his fate fince their laft parting,
explained the nature of his prefent fituation, and
concluded by declaring himfelf the happieft of
men.

THE Dervife attentively liftened to his difcourfe,
but did not feem to enter into his raptures. On
the contrary, affuming a feverity of afpect, " Such
(faid he) are the avocations allotted for thofe whom
nature hath formed with moderate intellects, to
move within the fhade of life ; but her extraordinary talents are beftowed for other purpofes of
a higher

a higher order ; to improve the neceſſary arts, de-
viſe laws, extend commerce, conduct armies, aſſiſt in moving the machine of government, and
contrive patriot plans for the benefit of ſociety.
Believe me, ſon, this retreat is criminal : Providence hath deſigned you for the ſervice of the public. I bluſh to think you have been ſo eaſily diſ-
couraged from the honourable purſuit in which
you was engaged. You muſt forthwith quit this
favourite privacy, and relinquiſh theſe pleaſures,
which ſerve only to enervate the faculties of the
ſoul. To-morrow I will lead you back to the
hill of Akaba, which you ſhall aſcend by an ave-
nue oppoſite to that which you have attempted in
vain ; and, before we part, you ſhall be ſupplied
with ſuch armour as will enſure ſucceſs." Theſe
words acted like a charm upon the heart of Omrah, in which all the ideas of ambition revived. He
deſired he might be led forthwith to the trial ; and
the Derviſe, unwilling to baulk his inclination, ſet
out with him upon his journey by moon-light.

THE ſun had not yet gilded the hemiſphere, when
they arrived at the foot of the mountain. The
aſcent, though ſteep, was not of itſelf very dangerous : the caſtle appeared diſtinct to the eye ;
and a great number of individuals were ſeen
climbing towards it with the utmoſt eagerneſs and
induſtry :

induftry : but every minute was fatal to one or
other of thefe adventurers, who were oppofed
and attacked by irregular bands of formidable ruf-
fians, that overfpread the greater part of the hill
from top to bottom, having nothing elfe in view
but the ruin of thofe they encountered. As often
as their weapons took effeɔ̃t, the unhappy fufferer
loſt his footing, and rolled down with incredible
velocity into a dark and difmal gulph below, in
which he funk never to rife again. In order to
defend Omrah from the aſſault of thefe hideous
freebooters, the Dervife cafed him in a coat of mail
fo exquifitely tempered, that neither lance nor arrow, fcymetar nor mace, could make the leaſt im-
preſſion upon its furface. At the fame time he
armed him with a two-edged fword, fo fharp and
fhining, that no mortal fubſtance could refiſt its
edge, and no eye endure its fplendour.

THUS armed, he embraced his counfellor, and
fprang forwards with a look of confidence and
alacrity. The firſt infult he received was from
his former fellow-travellers, the tall changeling
and his lame tutor, who now occupied the lower
part of the declivity. They exhibited no figns of
recognition at fight of their old acquaintance, but
ran towards him with hoſtile intent. The tutor
ſtriking at him with his fcymetar miſſed his aim,
                                                    and

and the weapon defcended upon his own toe, which it fevered from the joint. The junior brandifhed his pole to as little purpofe; for it fwung harmlefs over the head of Omrah, who neverthelefs found himfelf not a little difconcerted by the found of the curfed rattle, which had once been to him fo pro-ductive of mifchief and misfortune.

HAVING fafely paffed thefe affociates, he was next encountered by a figure of a hideous afpect, meagre, wan, and yellow; with a fquinting blood-fhot eye, and deep indented frown, betokening a gloomy mix-ture of doubt, anxiety, and rage but ill fuppref-fed. His left hand held a halter, and his right was laid upon the pommel of his fword, while he ad-vanced in a menacing pofture, attended by an af-faffin with a dagger and dark lanthorn, and a ma-niac in his paroxyfm of frenzy, clanking his chains, and gnafhing his teeth. Their appearance was very dreadful; but their threats they did not en-deavour to execute. The foremoft of the three ftopped fhort at a fmall diftance from Omrah; and waving with his hand to reftrain his followers, contented himfelf with eyeing the youth earneftly as he paffed.

THE third groupe was headed by an ⁴old hoary hag, naked to the middle: her fkin was tawny, loofe, and wrinkled: her cheek-bones projected

projeated outwards, and helped to form an hollow
pit for her eyes, which were scarce visible ; her
mouth, extended from ear to ear, was furnished with
teeth as sharp as needles ; and these she always dif-
closed like a dog that snarls. Her scalding tears
had fretted deep channels on her face, which was
a lively expression of rancour and anguish. Her
bloated dugs, that hung down to her waist, were
fore and cankered ; yielding, instead of milk, a
constant distillation of poison, which tortured her
so severely, that she shrieked aloud at every drop
that fell from the nipple. This was carefully col-
leaed by some of her attendants in two earthen
cups, in which they dipped the arrows they shot at
her command. In her hands she held two living
snakes, that twined round her arms, and seemed
to exasperate her torments with the most hideous
hissing. Her troop consisted of a motley crew, as
different in their garb as various in their occupations. One tainted the air by diffusing his enve-
nomed breath in whispers, shaking the head, shrug-
ging the shoulders, pointing with the finger, and
practising a thousand antic gesticulations. Another with inflated cheeks, and hoarse discordant
voice, poured forth a torrent of obloquy, and from
a basket slung before him, pelted our youth with
balls of filth and ordure. A third rushed forward
in the garb of a juggler, with a grinning mask

upon

upon his face, an oftrich feather in his right hand, and in his left a pair of affes ears, which he endeavoured to fix upon the head of Omrah. He feemed to have no language of his own; but counterfeited a vaft variety of founds peculiar to different animals. He mewed like a cat, roared like a lion, lowed like a camel, and howled like a dog : but he performed no part fo naturally, as that of braying like an afs. He laughed and whimpered, fcolded and fung, danced like a Marabout, and halted like a cripple. He practifed a thoufand ludicrous poftures, and attempted to tickle the throat of Omrah with his feather : but the youth, with his fword in the fcabbard, kept him ftill at a diftance. He had much more to apprehend from the archers of this infernal band, who ftood behind their fellows, and plied him with their poifoned arrows from every quarter. Nothing could have faved him from the points of thefe miffiles, but the mail he had received from the Dervife, in confequence of which he perfevered in his afcent.

The laft antagonift that took the field againft him, appeared in the habit of an Iman, huge in ftature, grave, fleek, and folemn ; with a fixed unmeaning eye, and an air of fupercilious contempt. A large owl perched on each fhoulder; and he grafped with both hands a leaden mace, which he

raifed

raifed againft our adventurer, while the two birds of Athens flapped their wings, and fcreeched with horrid utterance. Omrah was difcompofed at fight of this gigantic adverfary ftalking towards him with uplifted arm, and deliberated with himfelf whether he fhould remain on the defenfive, or pre- pare for battle. He had not yet determined, when his enemy directing a blow with all his force, the youth nimbly flipped afide, and the momentum of the ftroke brought the unwieldy Iman to the ground. The hill being fteep in this place, he rolled down ten paces, until he was ftopped by a kind of natural terrace; where he lay in a dif- graceful attitude, with his pofteriors expofed to the derifion of all paffengers.

Omrah had now paffed unhurt through all hoftilities, and afcended to the fummit of the hill, when he perceived the caftle furrounded with a wall of ice, the cold emanations of which began to pierce him to the marrow. Cafting his eyes around, he beheld the ground ftrewed with the bodies of thofe, who, after having furmounted all the other dangers and difficulties of the hill, had been frozen by the influence of this icy mound; and, in order to avoid the fame fate, he haftened to his laft refource. He already began to feel his blood creeping flow; and his teeth chattered in

his

his head, before he could unsheath the enchanted sword of Merit: but this no sooner gleamed upon the battlements, than they melted like snow beneath the noon-day sun; and he entered in triumph through the breach it had made.

WITHIN the court he beheld Hazima on his throne; and the lustre of the sword having flashed in the eyes of that minister, he beckoned Omrah towards him with a gracious smile. " Son (said he), you have gloriously passed your probation: and now it is my duty to reward your virtue." So saying, he seated him at his right hand: and the place of his chief secretary being vacant, he was forthwith invested with that office. Next day, Hazima presented him to the khaliph; and, in a few months, he insinuated himself into the favour of that mighty emperor.

FORTUNE had now recompensed him for all his sufferings; but it was not in her power to intoxicate his fancy, or in the least impair the virtues of his heart; which seemed to increase in proportion to the means he had of exercising them. Wealth flowed in upon him from every quarter; and this he again discharged in a thousand different channels, planned by his sagacity, and filled by his benevolence.

PASSING

PASSING one night through a bazar near the gate El Maazan, he perceived a number of flaves, chained together, ftanding for fale; and among the reft, a tall female, covered with a veil; which he lifted up in order to gratify his curiofity: but what were the emotions of his heart, when he beheld the features of his adorable Fatima! He was ftruck dumb with a tranfport of joyful furprize; while the fame paffions operated in her tender bofom with nearly the fame effect. "Have I then found thee (cried he), thou ineftimable jewel of my heart? Now fhall my happinefs be pure without alloy." At this addrefs, her eyes lightened with pleafure; while fhe pronounced thefe words: " Allah be praifed, that I once more behold thee unchanged in fentiment and affection! I have never fmiled fince our laft parting; but fighed inceffantly, and made continual excurfions in hopes of feeing thee again.—Providence has bleffed my endeavours. I and thefe my attendants were yefterday furrounded and taken by a body of the khaliph's gingulile, who have brought us hither for fale: and Allah, no doubt, fent thee hither for our relief."

OMRAH inftantly paid the purchafe for Fatima and her companions; and conducted them in perfon to his own houfe, where his miftrefs

was

was treated with all the delicacy of the moſt
reſpectful love. As their hearts were mutually
warmed with the moſt tender affection, he reſolved to be joined to her by the ſolemn nuptial
vow; and communicated his deſign to his pa-
tron Hazima, who expreſſed a deſire of ſeeing this
amiable captive. The requeſt was not altogether
ſuitable to the Moſlem cuſtoms; nevertheleſs, it
was granted by Omrah, in conſideration of Hazima's age and character. After ſupper, Fatima
made her appearance; and the old treaſurer was
confounded at her beauty. She was gorgeouſly
arrayed for the occaſion; and, among other or-
naments, wore on her right arm a remarkable
bracelet, decked with the precious ſtones called
turquoiſes. Hazima, having eyed this jewel and
the wearer by turns, with the moſt eager attention, ſuddenly ſtarted up, the tears running over
his ſnowy beard, and exclaimed in the utmoſt
agitation, " Holy prophet! is not this Abbaſſah,
the darling child of my old age, who was ſtolen
by a party of Curdes in her infancy from my ſummer reſidence in the neighbourhood of Caruſara?
Look, if that bracelet contains not a portion of
hair, with the cypher of her mother, the fair
Fadlrouah."

AT

AT this exclamation, Omrah ftood motion-
lefs, fixed in amazement and expectation: but
Fatima, fluſhed with ſtrong emotion, inſtantly
unbound the bracelet, and preſented it on her knee
to the treaſurer; who, having recognized the cypher, clafped her in his arms, and cried, " She
is—ſhe is my long-loſt Abbaſſah." With the
ſtreams that bedewed his face ſhe mingled the
tears of joy and filial affection, even while her
heart was too big for utterance.

OMRAH did not ſee this ſcene unmoved. His
joy was daſhed with apprehenſion, and he kneeled
in anxious fuſpence before the knees of Hazima,
who now, recollecting himſelf, took his daughter
by the hand, and delivered it to her enraptured
lover. He received her as the beſt gift of Providence, and kiſſed in acknowledgement the hem
of Hazima's garment. The day was appointed
for their ſpoufals, which were folemnized with
great magnificence; and Omrah lived to be
diſtinguiſhed by the epithet of " The Happy
Moſlem."

E S S A Y III.

IN that diſtrict of Greenland on the weſtern coaſt diſtinguiſhed by the name of Amaralek, lived two remarkable perſonages, called SIBBERSIK and IGLUKA; the former deemed the moſt accompliſhed youth that ever worſhipped the great *Torngarſuk on this ſide of the inſurmountable icy ridge that runs acroſs the country, whether in twanging the elaſtic bow of Tenal, launching the dart, hurling the harpoon, paddling the canoe, or diving under water to ſcoop the blubber from the back of the expiring whale; and ſhe univerſally allowed to excel all the nymphs of Greenland in beauty and rare qualifications, as much as the moon excels the aurora borealis in light and ſplendor. She was daughter and ſole heireſs of the †Angekuk Ajokarſorpok, one of the wealthieſt of all the Greenland patriarchs. He poſſeſſed

* Torngarſuk is a miſchievous deity worſhipped by the Greenlanders.

† Angekuks are the heads of the clergy, the lawgivers, the nobles, and the prophets of Greenland.

two kone boats, five canoes, three huge piles of
wood for rafts poles boards and fewel, feven chefts
of brafs copper and tin utenfils, purchafed from
the * Kublunæts, a fpacious winter cabin, a magnificent fummer tent, and a vaft magazine well
filled with blubber, whalebone, morfe teeth, uni-
corns horns, the fkins of fox, feal, and rein-deer.

His darling Igluka had been bred up in the
utmoft tendernefs and elegance. Her fhift appeared white and tranfparent, being formed of
the maw of holibut : her waiftcoat was of the
fofteft faun-fkin, trimmed with white by her own
fair hands : the fkin of the rein-deer fupplied her
with an upper garment and hood; and her
breeches and boots were formed of a dreffed feal-
fkin, foft fmooth and pliant. This was her ordinary drefs : but on feftivals fhe wore a magnificent robe of bird's fkin, adorned with variegated
feathers, and bracelets fet with pearls. Her locks,
that emulated the raven's back, were nicely braid-
ed : her gloffy neck was hung round with beads
of glafs and coral. Her eyes glanced like the
three ftars in the belt of Sicktut †. Her teeth, in
whitenefs, rivalled the fnow that covers the moun-

* Kublunæts, the name given to the Danes by the Greenlanders.

† Sicktut is the appellation by which the Greenlanders
diftinguifh the conftellation Orion.

tains

tains of Nepſet; and ſhe ſmelled ſo ſweet of virgin water, that ſhe never went forth without receiving the ſalutation Niviarſiarſuanerks *.   She
repoſed upon beds of eider-down ; and was every
day carefully anointed with the fat of the whale's
belly. She fed upon the eggs of ſea-fowl gathered among the cliffs, upon the rogn-fiſh ; the tail
of young whales delicately ſauced with train-oil ;
the fleſh of ſea-calves ; the raſpings of ſeal-ſkin
made into pancakes ; the ingeſta and chawdron of
the rein-deer ; the entrails of the rype or partridge
dreſſed with blubber ; and, by way of deſſert, the
ſea-weed and the root called tugloronet, ſliced and
fried with train-oil.

A YOUNG lady of ſuch expectations, nurſed
with indulgence, and trained up in the midſt
of ſuch delicacies, could not but be inſpired
with the moſt refined ſentiments, and ſo animated by the pride of birth, as well as by the
conſciouſneſs of her own beauty and accompliſh-
ments, as to look down with contempt upon the
generality of thoſe youths who aſpired to her good
graces.   Indeed it was univerſally believed, that
ſhe would chooſe to lead a life of celibacy rather
than beſtow herſelf in marriage upon any indivi-

* Niviarſiarſuane:ks ſignifies, " how ſhe ſmells like a
virgin!" and is applied to thoſe who ſprinkle themſelves
with their own water.

D 2   dua

dual of Amaralek: but fate had otherwife ordained in favour of the gallant Sibberfik, who was not only rich in the goods of fortune, but alfo excelled all his cotemporaries in beauty, courage, and agility, as well as in the gifts of the underftanding. He had flain a mighty bear in fingle combat, and in winter wore the fkin acrofs his fhoulders, as a trophy of his victory. He had once ventured to affault the dreadful fea monfter Hafgufa *, and was the firft who had ever efcaped with life from fuch a rencounter. He had often dived beneath the ice, in purfuit of feals and morfes; and in the moft dreadful tempefts put to fea in his flender canoe of bended fticks covered with fkins. His dart and harpoon flew unerring to the mark; and his arrows never miffed the fea-mew upon the cliff, or the rein-deer on the mountain. He never failed to win the prize at foot-ball, catch-ball, wreflling and dancing; and far outfhone all his companions in the poetical contefts of alternate fatire, practifed at public feftivals among the fwains of Greenland †.

THE fair Igluka could notbe infenfible to all thefe perfections. She took pleafure in feeing him

* Hafgufa is fuppofed to be a fpirit that appears at fea to the Greenlanders, in many different hideous forms.

† The youths of Greenland actually contend in this manner, like the ancient fwains of Arcadia.

perform

perform all his feats of ſtrength and activity; and
always rewarded him for the victory he had obtained, ſometimes with a ſmile and ſometimes with
a preſent.   After a ſevere trial of wreſtling, ſhe
once refreſhed him with a draught of train-oil; at
another time ſhe preſented him with a ſpring coat
of ſeal-ſkin, cut and ſewed by her own delicate
fingers; but the favour which of all others he
moſt eſteemed, and which brought upon him the
envy of all his companions, was an invitation ſhe
gave him to ſup with her on the leg of a frozen
ſeal, and the ſound of a hay-fiſh ſtewed in blubber:
nay, to crown his good fortune, after this genial
banquet, ſhe licked him * all over, that he might
derive double vigour from this unction of maiden
ſpittle; and inveſted him with a ſhift of ſeal gut?,
which for that purpoſe ſhe ſtripped from her own
delicate body.   In a word, Igluka and Sibberſik
had by this time captivated the hearts of each
other.   The rocks reſounded with the ſongs which
he compoſed in her praiſe.   He formed garlands
of ſea-weeds intermixed with ſhells and corals for
her hair: he made her an offering of the firſt-fruits
of all his labours; and ſeized all opportunities of
whiſpering in her ears the moſt delicate and endearing expreſſions of love.

* This practice, which was probably learned from the
bear's licking her cubs, is common in Greenland.

IN the midft of this tender communication, the good old Ajokarforpok was gathered to his fathers, and the lovely Igluka rema·ned fole miftrefs of his whole eftate. Sibberfik continued to enjoy all the awful privileges of a favoured lover, and at length the day was fixed for uniting this accomplifhed pair in the filken bands of Hymen. Meanwhile they fet out together on the fummer's expedition of deer-hunting : they ate from the fame platter, they flept in the fame tent, and conftantly accompanied each other in all the evolutions of the chace. Such an intimacy between the two fexes is often productive of the moft fatal confequences, which even the pureft fentiments and the moft determined virtue cannot always prevent. The moft perfect nature and the moft cautious honour have their unguarded moments; and in one of thefe the amiable, the elegant, the virtuous, the fentimental Igluka was undone.

AFTER the fatigue of the chace, Sibberfik fpread his bear-fkin for the repofe of his beauteous miftrefs under a projecting rock, whofe foot was lafhed by the refounding wave. The noife of the billows, and the clattering of the ice, foon lulled her into an agreeable flumber. The lover lay down by her fide : he prefled her to his bofom ; waked her gently with the

foft

foft murmurs of his paffion ; and made fuch artful ufe of the opportunity, that in an evil hour
fhe furrendered up her virgin treafure, while the
fea-mews and curlieus fcreamed, the bears growl-
ed, and feals grunted in concert, as if to celebrate
thefe portentous rites. In Sibberfik enjoyment was
foon followed with fatiety; his fondnefs vifibly
abated; he relaxed in his attention and affiduity;
he engaged in feparate parties from his charmer;
he avoided her habitation and fociety; and finally
refufed to perform the folemn vow by means of
which he had triumphed over her virginity.

It may well be imagined what effect thefe inftances of flight and perfidy in the man fhe loved,
had upon a young lady of fuch rank and fenfibility. She found herfelf deprived of her honour,
and the fymptoms of her difgrace waxing fo vifi-
ble, that it would not be in her power to conceal it
much longer.   Thefe confiderations filled her
breaft with horrour, and thrice fhe refolved to
bury herfelf and her misfortunes in a watery grave:
but as often as fhe attempted to execute this dire
refolve, fhe heard, or feemed to hear, a voice that
pronounced the following words, *Torngarfungnut
makko ineille pegomnagit* *; which in the language
of Greenland fignifies, " Take heed left thou

* Vide Egede's Hiftory of Greenland.

" go

D

" go to the devil." Thus deterred from laying
violent hands on her own life, she began to pine
away in solitude, indulging her grief, and giving
up herself to the moft bitter defpair. The luftre
vanifhed from her eyes, and the fhining glofs
forfook her countenance : her jetty locks hung
difhevelled ; and no more fhe bedewed herfelf
with the odoriferous virgin-ftream ; for alas!
this was no longer in her power. No more fhe
indulged her appetite with the choiceft cates ; but
fometimes, to fupport her drooping fpirits, fhe
comforted herfelf with a cup of oil, thick, yellow, and perfumed. In a word, while her middle increafed in circumference, the reft of her
body wafted apace ; and her relations forefaw,
that in a little time fhe would in all probability
be conveyed to her grave, with her thimbles and
needles, and wearing apparel.

SIBBERSIK was not ignorant of her condition,
nor infenfible of the injury he had done to this accomplifhed young lady : but poffeffion had palled
upon his fenfe, and his love was fuccecded by a fpecies of difguft, which neither his honour nor his
reafon could overcome. Neverthelefs, they ftrug-
gled fo hard in behalf of the forfaken Igluka, as to
banifh all tranquillity from his bofom. The diverfions he purfued, no longer yielded him the leaft
enjoyment ;

enjoyment; the occupations in which he engaged, were incapable of screening him from the horrors of confcience; and the converfation of his friends acted like poifon to his thought. He, in his turn, neglected his food and apparel, became penfive and melancholy, and the only relief which he felt was in fixing himfelf in his canoe, and launching into the deep, that he might lofe the fenfe of his own internal tempefts, amidft the loudeft ftorms that dafhed upon the rocks of Greenland. In thefe excurfions his imagination was often haunted by the fea-fpirit Ingnerfort *, which fometimes rofe before him in the fhape of a mermaid, and fometimes made the caverns of the fhore refound with the moft difmal fhrieking. He looked upon thefe vifitations as prefages of his death ; and even feemed to welcome his approach towards the land of fpirits. One day his frail canoe was bulged upon an ifland of ice ; and with the utmoft difficulty he, by fwimming, gained the fhore at the very place where he had deflowered the unfortunate Igluka.

THE review of the fatal fpot conjured up the idea of his guilt with all the circumftances of aggravation. He fmote his breaft in defpair; and

* The common fea-fprite of Greenland is known by this name.

that inftant a huge feal, ftarting from the in-
terior part of the cave, paffed him grunting, and
plunged into the fea. He never doubted but this
was the fpirit Torngarfuk, which pronounced
the funereal word Picklerrukput *, as an omen of
his fate. He endeavoured to flay this mifchie-
vious fiend by an eruption of wind backwards,
the only charm, which, according to the Greenland mythology, the devil cannot refift † :   but,
notwithftanding the prevalency of his fear, he
found it impoffible to try the experiment.   His
hair briftled up, his knees knocked together, and
he fell down in a trance upon the fated fcene of
his difhonour.

HAVING lain for fome time infenfible, he recovered the ufe of his faculties, and found himfelf in the prefence of a famous Angekuk or
prophet, who, being made acquainted with his
cafe, admonifhed him fo effectually, that he re-
newed his addreffes to the poor forlorn Igluka.
Such an unexpected return of happinefs foon re-

* This phrafe, fignifying " Here is no more to be
got," the next of kin pronounces at the deceafe of a
Greenlander.

† Such is really the notion which the Greenlanders entertain of this deity.

ftored

ſtored her to her former health and ſpirits: the
two lovers were happily united by the prieſt:
in two months after the wedding, which was celebrated with great magnificence, Igluka brought
forth a pair of lovely boys, and ſhe and her huſ-
band paſſed their lives in a continual round of
conjugal felicity.

D 6   E S S A Y

E S S A Y IV.

A LCANOR was the fon of a London merchant, bred up to the bufinefs of his father,.
to which he fucceeded in his early youth; and in
a little time diftinguifhed himfelf not only by his
knowledge in trade, but alfo by his probity of
heart and generofity of fentiment. Nor was he
deficient in perfonal accomplifhments : his figure
was remarkably agreeable ; his addrefs was engaging ; and no pains had been fpared in giving him.
the advantage of a genteel education.

. HE was in a fair way of acquiring a very large
fortune, when he firft beheld, at a public aflembly,
the elegant and amiable EUDOSIA, daughter of an
eminent trader, to whom his circumftances were
well known. He was deeply ftruck with her external appearance; and having found means to in-
finuate himfelf into her acquaintance, difcovered
a thoufand charms in her underftanding and difpofition, which at once completed the conqueft of
his heart. It was not long before he difclcfed his

                                                passion.

paffion to the dear object, and had the ravifhing pleafure to find he had infpired her with very favourable fentiments of his character.

AFTER fome time fpent in the endearing effufions of mutual love, he applied to the father, and made a formal demand of her in marriage. His propofal met with a very cordial reception ; and Alcanor was admitted into the family on the footing of a future fon-in-law. The day was already appointed for the marriage, after all the articles of intereft had been fettled to the fatisfaction of both parties, when, by the fudden failure of foreign correfpondents at the clofe of the laft war, Alcanor was obliged to ftop payment. He communicated his diftrefs to Eudofia's father ; and produced his books, by which it appeared that his effects were more than fufficient to difcharge his debts ; though they were fo fcattered, that he could not call them in time enough to fupport his credit. The merchant faid he was forry for his misfortune, but made no offer of affiftance : on the contrary, he told him bluntly, that he could not expect he would beftow his daughter on a bankrupt, and forbade him the houfe. The reader may conceive what an effect this treatment had upon an ingenuous mind, endued with an extraordinary fhare of fenfibility : he retired to his own houfe, his heart burfting with grief and indignation.

THE

THE generous Eudofia, being apprifed of what had
paffed between her father and her lover, feized the
firft opportunity of writing a letter to Alcanor, lamenting his misfortune in the moft pathetic terms;
affuring him of her inviolable attachment, and
offering to give a convincing proof of her love by
a clandeftine marriage.   He made due acknow-
ledgements to his amiable miftrefs for this mark
of her difintereftled affection; but abfolutely refufed to comply with a propofal which might ruin
her fortune, endanger her happinefs, and fubject
him to the imputation of being fordid and felfifh.
He made hafte to fettle his accounts, and fatisfy
his creditors.   Then he wrote a letter to Eudofia,
releafing her from all engagements in his favour,
and exhorting her to forget that ever any fuch perfon exifted.   Immediately after this addrefs, he
difappeared, and no perfon could tell in what manner: people, in general, fuppofed he had made
away with himfelf in defpair.

EUDOSIA was overwhelmed with the moft poig-
nant forrow, which intailed upon her a lingering
diftemper, that brought her to the brink of the grave.
Though nature triumphed over the difeafe, it was not
in the power of time to remove her grief, which
fettled into a fixed melancholy that clouded all her
charms, and made a deep impreffion on her father's
heart.

heart. Her only brother dying of a confumption, fhe became the fole heirefs of a confiderable fortune ; and many advantageous matches were propofed without effect. At length, fhe plainly told her father, that he had once made her miferable, and it was not now in his power to make her happy ; for fhe had made a folemn vow to heaven, that fhe would never join her fate to any other man but him on whom he had allowed her to beftow her affection. The merchant was thunderftruck at this declaration; he faw himfelf deprived, by his own cruel avarice, of that happinefs, which he had flattered himfelf with the hope of enjoying in a rifing generation of his own pofterity: he became penfive and fullen; loft his fenfes ; and in a few months expired.

EUDOSIA purchafed a retired houfe in the country, where fhe gave a full fcope to her forrow, while fhe lived the life of a faint, and fpent the beft part of her time, as well as fortune, in the exercife of charity and benevolence : witnefs the fighs that are ftill uttered by all that knew her, when her name is pronounced : witnefs the tears of the widow and the fatherlefs, that are daily fhed upon her tomb.

ALCANOR, defperate in his fortune and his love, took a paffage in a Spanifh fhip for Cadiz,

under

under the name of Benfon ; and as he underftood the languages, as well as the management of ac-compts, he was admitted, as an inferior factor, on board of the Flota bound for South America.

HE fettled at La Vera Cruz ; and fortune fo prof-pered his endeavours, that, in a few years, he was mafter of forty thoufand piftoles. But neither profperity, nor the univerfal efteem he had ac-quired among the Spaniards for his worth and in-tegrity, could footh the anguifh of his heart, or efface the remembrance of Eudolia, whofe charms ftill dwelt upon his imagination. At length, im-patient of living fo long in ignorance of her fitua-tion, he remitted his effects to Europe, returned to Cadiz, and there in a Britifh bottom took fhip-ping for England. At the Race of Portland, the fhip was attacked by a paltry French privateer, and Alcanor had the misfortune to receive a fhot in his neck, which appeared very dangerous. After the privateer had fheered off, he defired that he might be put afhore at the neareft land, as there was no furgeon on board ; and the boat immedi-ately conveyed him and part of his baggage into a creek, within half a mile of Eudolia's dwelling. He was obliged to take up his lodging at a wretched public-houfe, and difpatched an exprefs to the next town for a furgeon ; but before he ar-rived, the unfortunate Alcanor had loft his eye-

fight,

fight, in confequence of his wound, and his fever was confiderably increafed.

THE humane Eudofia, being made acquainted
with the circumftances of his diftrefs, without
dreaming that it was her beloved Alcanor, defired a
worthy old clergyman, who was rector of the parifh,
to take her chariot, and bring the wounded gentleman to her houfe, where he might be properly attended and accommodated. Thither he was carried
accordingly, and there firft vifited by the furgeon,
who, after having dreffed the wound, declared he
had no hopes of his recovery. He heard this fentence without emotion ; and defired he might have
an opportunity to thank the lady of the houfe for
the charitable compaffion fhe had manifefted towards a ftranger in diftrefs.

THE tender-hearted Eudofia, being informed
of his requeft, immediately vifited him in his
apartment, accompanied by the clergyman, and a
female relation who lived with her as her companion. Approaching his bedfide, fhe condoled
with him on his misfortune, begged he would
think himfelf at home, and command every thing
in her houfe as freely as if it were his own. He
no fooner heard her voice than he ftarted ; and
raifing himfelf in his bed, rolled his eyes around as
if in queft of fome favourite object. His ear was
more

more faithful than his memory : he remembered
and was affected by the ftrain, though he could not
recollect the ideas to which it had been annexed :
after fome paufe he exclaimed, " Excellent lady !
I could wifh to live, in order to exprefs my gratitude : but it will not be.—You have given fhelter
to a poor wearied pilgrim ; and your charity muft
be ftill farther extended in feeing his body committed to the duft. I have, moreover, another favour to afk, namely, that you and this good clergyman will atteft my laft will, which is locked in
a paper-cafe depofited in my portmanteau." So
faying, he delivered the key to the doctor, who
opened the trunk, found the paper, and was defired to recite it aloud in the hearing of all prefent.

THE will was written by the hand of Alcanor
himfelf, who, in confideration of his tender affection for the incomparable Eudofia, which nothing,
but death fhould eraze from his heart, had bequeathed to her all his worldly fubftance, exclufive
of fome charitable legacies. When the name of
Alcanor was pronounced, Eudofia ftarted, grew
pale, and trembled with ftrong emotion : yet
fhe confidered his fituation, and reftrained her
tranfports, while her eyes poured forth a torrent
of tears, and the chair fhook under her with the
violence of her agony. The humane clergyman
was not unmoved at this fcene. He had often
heard.

heard the ftory of her unfortunate love, and by his fenfible confolations enabled her to bear her affliction with temper and refignation. He no fooner perceived the names of Alcanor and Eudofia in the will, than he was feized with extreme wonder, and fympathizing forrow. His voice faltered, the tears ran down his cheeks, and it was with the utmoft difficulty that he read the paper to an end. Then obferving the agitation of Eudofia, he conducted her into another room, where, her grief and furprize becoming too ftrong for her conftitution, fhe fainted away in the arms of her companion. When fhe recovered from this fwoon, fhe gave vent to her forrow in a loud paffion of tears and exclamation; after which fhe became more calm ; and begged the doctor would endeavour to prepare Alcanor for an interview with his long-loft Eudofia. He forthwith returned to the merchant ; but was in too much confufion to communicate the difcovery with difcretion and compofure.

Alcanor, though blind, had perceived the lady's agitation, as well as the clergyman's diforder, and was not a little furprifed at their abrupt departure. His mind had already formed an affemblage of the moft interefting ideas before the doctor returned ; and when he began to expatiate on the
myfterious

myfterious ways of Providence, he was interrupted by the ftranger, who, raifing his head, and clafping his hands, exclaimed aloud, " O bountiful Heaven ! it muft—it muft be the incomparable Eudofia !" At that inftant fhe entered the apartment, kneeled by the bed-fide, and taking him by the hand, " It is (cried fhe) the unfortunate Eudofia—O my Alcanor ! Is it thus we meet ?" A long filence enfued, during which he bathed her hand with his tears. -- At length he fpoke to this effect : " Thefe are not the tears of forrow, but of joy.— Eudofia then lives ! She remembers—fhe retains her regard for the haplefs Alcanor !—It was indeed the kind hand of Providence that threw me on this hofpitable fhore. — Could I once more behold thofe dear features which I have fo often contemplated with admiration and delight—but, I am fatisfied."——

The fequel of this affecting fcene I cannot pretend to defcribe.——Alcanor's wound at the next drefling had the appearance of a beginning gangrene : neverthelefs, the ball, which had been lodged among the nerves and finews of the neck, was now with eafe extracted, and his eye-fight was immediately reftored. Having fettled his temporal affairs, and made his peace with heaven, he on the fourth day expired in the arms

of

of Eudofia, who was the fole and laft object on which his eyes were ftrained.

SHE did not long furvive her unfortunate lover. Her grief at length exhaufted her conftitution, and brought her to the grave, after fhe had endowed alms-houfes for the maintenance of twenty poor cripples, bequeathed a handfome fortune to her kinfwoman, a confiderable prefent to the clergyman, and a large fum to the poor of the parifh. At her own defire fhe was buried in the fame grave with her lover, and over them is raifed a plain unembellifhed tomb of black marble, with this modeft infcription: " Dedicated to the memory of ALCANOR and " EUDOSIA."

E S S A Y V.

To *the* E D I T O R.

S I R,

I WAS much affected with the philofophical re-fignation of the honeft SOLDIER * who made his appearance in your MAGAZINE for JUNE (1760) and his ftory made the deeper impreffion upon my mind, as his difpofition forms a ftriking contraft with my own.

I WAS the fecond fon of a wealthy gentleman, who referved the bulk of his fortune for my elder brother ; fo that the only provifion I enjoyed, was, a tolerable education and a lieutenant's com-miffion in the army. During the late war I ob-tained a company by dint of fervice, and at the peace was reduced upon half-pay. But this re-duction was no great misfortune to me, who had learned to practife œconomy in an inferior ftation, and was fo much mafter of my accounts, that I

* See GOLDSMITH's ESSAYS, Vol. I. Effay xxiv. p. 203

could

could live independent even to my wifh, and could fave fomething out of the appointments of a re-formed captain.

My father having by this time refigned his breath, I had no parental home to which I could retire ; therefore I fet up my reft in a country town, where I had been formerly quartered with the regiment, and made fome agreeable acquaintances. There I paffed my time according to my heart's defire. I fifhed, fowled, and hunted with the gentlemen of the neighbourhood, who entertained me in their houfes with the moft cordial hofpitality. I walked, I chatted, I danced and played at cards with their wives and daughters. Delightful excurfions, and amufing parties of pleafure, were planned and executed every day. The time ftole away infen-fibly : I knew no care : I felt no diforder. I in-herited from nature a vigorous conftitution, a happy ferenity of temper, and was diftinguifhed among my friends as the beft-humoured fellow in the world.

In the midft of thefe enjoyments my heart was touched by the amiable qualities of a young lady, who was content to unite her fate with mine, con-trary to the inclination, and without the confent

of

of her father, who poſſeſſed a very large fortune,
and reſented her marriage with ſuch perſeverance
of indignation, that he never would admit her
into his preſence, nor even, at his death, forgive
her for the ſtep ſhe had taken. His diſpleaſure,
however, affected us the leſs, as we found happi-
neſs in our mutual paſſion, and knew no wants ;
for my wife inherited from an aunt a legacy of
eighteen hundred pounds, the intereſt of which,
together with my half-pay, was ſufficient to anſwer
all our occaſions.

WE found great ſatisfaction in contriving plans
for living ſnug upon our income, and enjoyed un-
ſpeakable pleaſure in executing the ſcheme to
which we had given the preference. Chance preſented us with an opportunity to purchaſe a ſmall,
though neat and convenient houſe, with about
twenty acres of land, in an agreeable rural ſitua-
tion ; and there our time was parcelled out in a
ſucceſſion of taſks, for improving a large farm
that we rented, and cultivating a ſweet little garden laid out on a gentle ſlope, the foot of which
was watered by a brawling rivulet of pure tranſparent water. Although Heaven had not thought
proper to indulge us with children, we were favoured with every other ſubſtantial bleſſing ; and
every circumſtance of rural œconomy proved a
ſource of health and ſatisfaction. The labours

of

of the field, the little domeftick cares of the barn-
yard, the poultry-yard, and the dairy, were productive of fuch delights as none of your readers
will conceive, except thofe who are enamoured of
a country-life. I cannot remember thofe peaceful
fcenes of innocence and tranquillity without re-
gret; they often haunt my imagination, like the
ghofts of departed happinefs. Within the bofom
of this charming retreat we lived, in a ftate of
uninterrupted enjoyment, until our felicity was
invaded by two unexpected events, at which, I
am afraid, we fhall always have caufe to repine:
my nephew, who had fucceeded to my father's
eftate, died of the fmall-pox, and, a few weeks
after this incident, my wife's only brother broke
his neck in leaping a five-barred gate: fo that we
found ourfelves, all at once, in poffeffion of a very
opulent fortune, and violently tranfported from
that element for which our tempers had been fo
well adapted.

In the firft flutter and agitation of mind occafioned by this unhoped-for acceffion, we quitted
our romantic folitude, and rufhed into all the
pageantry of high-life. Thus irrefiftibly fucked
within the vortex of Diffipation, we grew giddy in
a rapid whirl of unnatural diverfion: we became
enamoured of tinfel liveries, equipage, and all the

frippery of fafhion. Inftead of tranquillity, health, a continual flow of fatisfaction, and a fucceffion of rational delights, which we formerly derived from temperance, exercife, the ftudy of nature, and the practice of benevolence, we now tafted no pleafure but what confifts in the gratification of idle vanity, toffed for ever on a fea of abfurd amufements by fuch loud ftorms of riot and tumult, as drowned the voice of reafon and reflection, and overwhelmed all the beft faculties of the foul. We deferted nature, fentiment, and true tafte, to lead a weary life of affectation, folly, and intemperance; our fenfes became fo depraved, that our eyes were captivated with glare and glitter, and our ears with noife and clamour; while our fancy dwelt with pleafure on every gewgaw of Gothic extravagance. We entertained guefts whom we defpifed, we vifited friends whom we did not love, and invited company whom we could not efteem. We drank wines that we could not relifh, and ate victuals which we could not digeft. We frequented concerts which we did not underftand, plays that we did not like, and public diverfions which we could not enjoy. Our houfe might have been termed the Temple of Uproar: card-tables were the fhrines, and the votaries feemed agitated by the dæmons of envy, fpite, rage, vexation and defpair. In a word, all was farce and form,—all was a

phantafma,

phantafma, and a hideous dream of incoherent abfurdities.

THESE pleafures, like brandy to a dram-drink-
er, have loft their effect; we have waked from
the intoxication to a due fenfe of our miferable
condition; for the vigour both of mind and body
is quite impaired. With refpect to each other,
we find ourfelves in a ftate of mutual difguft; and
all the enjoyments of life we either tafte with in-
difference, or reject with loathing. For my own
part, I am overwhelmed with what the French
call *l'ennui*, a diftemper for which there is no
name in the Englifh language; a diftemper which
may be underftood from the following lines of
the poet :

> Thee too, my Paridel, fhe faw thee there,
> Stretch'd on the rack of a too eafy chair ;
> And heard thy everlafting yawn confefs
> The pains and penalties of idlenefs.

IT is not a common vacancy of thought, or an
ordinary languor of the nerves that I labour under, but a confirmed imbecility of mind, and a
want of relifh, attended with a thoufand uneafi-
neffes which render life almoft infupportable. I
fleep without refrefhment ; I am fatigued without
labour. I am fcarce rifen when I wifh the day

was done, and when night comes I long for morning. I eat without appetite, drink without exhilaration; exercife affords no fpirits, conver-fation no amufement, reading no entertainment, and diverfion no pleafure. It is not from affectation, but an acquired infenfibility, that I fee Fal-ftaff without a fmile, and The Orphan without emotion. I endeavour to kill the time by fhifting continually the fcene of diffipation ; but I am clofe purfued by difguft : all is difappointment, infipid, naufeous, or fhocking. My temper is grown fo fretful and peevifh, that I quarrel by turns with my fervants and myfelf ; even fhe that was once the delight of my eyes, and the joy of my heart, is now become the fubjeft of perpetual difquiet. I harbour wifhes which I dare not approve ; my heart palpitates with paffions which I am afhamed to avow. I am tormented by a thoufand petty grievances, which rife like angry pimples from the ebullitions of a foured difpofition ; and incidents that would move the mirth of other men, are to me produftive of choler and anxiety. Two days ago I ordered my fervants to horfe-whip a cobler, who refufed to leave off whiftling in his ftall as he fat at work oppofite to my chamber-window ; and if I had then met with your maimed Soldier, in all probability I fhould have chaftifed him for pre-fuming to be more happy than his betters.

SIR,

SIR, if you have any recipe for the cure of my diforder, it will be charity to publifh it for the benefit of many thoufands that labour under the fame malady which now afflicts your humble fervant,

PICROMACHUS,

THE diftemper of our correfpondent is endemial among the Great, and may be termed a fcurvy of the fpirits. Exercife is as neceffary to the mind as to the body, and mental exercife confifts in ftudy and reflection: this being long difufed, the powers of reafon lofe their tone; and a relaxation of the nerves from idlenefs and furfeit, co-operating with this languor, the whole machine is, as it were, unftrung; all the faculties being thus untwifted and out of tune, the mind jars on every ftring, and nothing can be produced but difcord and difquiet. If PICROMACHUS and his Lady are really determined, if poffible, to obtain a radical cure, and retrieve their good-humour, let them make over to the next heirs the great eftates which devolved to them fo unexpectedly, and return to the farm with the fame neceffities which their own induftry had before fo happily fupplied. Should this be an effort of felf-denial beyond the pitch of their refolution, we would advife them to renounce their fafhionable connections, and endea-

vour to contract friendfhips with a few rational
creatures; to difmifs their fuperfluous fervants,
including the French cook, and every gaudy ap-
purtenance of oftentation; to retire from London,
and engage in the avocations of hufbandry; to ufe
the cold bath every morning, ride twenty miles
every day before dinner, eat moderately of plain
Englifh food, go to bed by eleven, rife before
eight, and faft one day in the week, until their
appetites are perfectly reftored.

ESSAY

ESSAY VI.

HOWSOEVER we may pride ourfelves on the refinements of the prefent age, we are not fo far removed from barbarifm as people in general imagine. It would be eafy to demonftrate, that every circumftance of the prefent fafhion is a fhocking outrage againft common fenfe, which is founded upon eternal truth, the bafis of all tafte and beauty; and it would be no difficult tafk to prove, that we are as Gothic in thofe fentiments of the heart which influence our conduct, as in the fuggeftions of the fancy that regulate the mode of our external appearance. Notwithftanding the pride and felf-complacency of thofe fluttering animals who call themfelves Perfons of Diftinction, roll in their triumphal chariots, and look down with difdain on their fellow-citizens as the dregs of the creation, they are no other than mere ruftics in point of true tafte and genuine politenefs, which are the natural effects of fenfibility and humanity, improved by knowlege; whereas the prefent mode is an un-

natural

natural monfter, begot upon the hag Ignorance
by her own fon the ideot Caprice; and what we
falfely term Good-breeding, is no other than the
fpurious brood of unfeeling Infolence and aukward Grimace. Thefe ridiculous perverfions derive their firft origin from error, and will never
be rectified, until the world fhall adopt a fyftem
of education quite different from that which at
prefent prevails. Very few pretend to think for
themfelves, but, in matters of tafte, implicitly
follow, like fimple fheep, certain Bell-weathers
of the fafhion, who are infligated by the dæmons
of Arrogance and Folly. In order to effect a reformation, it will be neceffary, that individuals
fhall exert their own faculties of reafon, and renounce thofe diftracted guides, whenever they
perceive them deviate from the road of nature
and of truth : but the faculty of judging cannot
be properly exerted, until it has been duly exercifed; and, for this purpofe, we ought to contrive proper objects of argument and reflection.
For my own part, as the bufinefs is to invefligate
truth, I would propofe the ftudy of geometry to
the youth of both fexes. After mifs hath finifhed
the letters of the A B C, let her begin a new
fampler for the Propofitions of Euclid. No young
lady fhould be admitted to a card-table, except by
croffing the *Pons Afinorum; nor prefide at an

* A Propofition fo called.

assembly,

affembly, until fhe could demonftrate the famous
Pythagorean difcovery, that the fquare of the hy-
pothenufe is equal to the fquares of the two
other fides in a right-angled triangle.   Every body
knows with what fuccefs mathematical reafoning
has been introduced into medicine : an ingenious
philofopher of our own day hath ufed the fame
fcience in determining the momenta with which
the paffions act upon the human mind : the Line
of Beauty difcovered by the celebrated Hogarth,
what is it but a mathematical curve? the charms
of painting, fculpture, and architecture, that ftrike
the fpectator's eye with irrefiftible energy, are
no other than a happy fymmetry of parts, that
may be refolved into mathematical relations : even
mufic itfelf is founded on mathematical proportion, and doubtlefs the fame rules of analytical
inveftigation may be applied in difcovering and
afcertaining the characters of mankind ; at leaft,
the ftudy of geometry will fix the attention of
the moft volatile female, teach her to think with
propriety, compare with caution, and judge with
precifion.

I was led into this train of thought by an incident which lately fell under my obfervation, at
one of thofe Medicinal Wells which, every fummer, attract a concourfe of what is called fafhion-

able people. A certain lady of quality, as remarkable for her good-fenfe as for her generofity of
temper, coming one day into the public room,
invited all the company then prefent to a ball at
her own houfe, intended for the next evening.
The guefts affembled accordingly ; and, that no
difputes might arife, the diftribution of partners
was left to the determination of chance : the gentlemen drew numbers out of one hat, the ladies
from another, and the two that correfponded were
coupled for the evening. The number 10 fell to
the fhare of a lady, who, underftanding that fhe
had drawn for her partner a young phyfician,
made no fecret of expreffing her diffatisfaction,
and even declared that fhe would not dance : the
poor doctor, ignorant of her chagrin, and as yet a
ftranger to his fate, went round the room, en-
quiring which of the ladies had drawn the number
10, and began to be much mortified at finding
himfelf un-owned. The lady of the ball, perceiving his fituation, acted with a delicacy peculiar to herfelf: fhe communicated her inftructions to her own daughter (whom we fhall call
CLARINDA), an amiable young lady and a reigning
toaft, who had drawn the fame number with a
gaudy officer that flaunted about the room in fcarlet
and embroidery. Clarinda, addreffing herfelf to
the difcontented nymph, begged as a favour that
they

they might exchange numbers, and her propofal
was greedily embraced: then this lovely creature,
blooming with all the graces of youth, beauty,
and good-nature, went up to the phyfician, and,
finiling ineffably fweet, told him fhe had the pleafure to be his partner for the evening. The doctor's eyes fparkled at her approach: his good fortune was envied by all the gentlemen; her conduct was applauded by the majority of the ladies;
and before the ball ended, the perfon by whom he
had been rejected was heartily afhamed of her filly
pride.

THAT the reader may be the better judge
of her choice, I fhall analyfe the two individuals
who ftood fo differently in her eftimation. The
phyfician was in his perfon tall, and elegantly
formed, with an open prepoffeffing countenance, a
modeft deportment, and engaging addrefs: the
officer was fhort, fquat, hard-favoured, clumfy, im-
pudent, and boorifh. The doctor defcended from
an honourable family; his rival was the fon of an
excifeman: the firft had expended a large fum on
his education, travelled for improvement, and laid
up an uncommon ftock of erudition; the other
wrote a good hand, underftood a little of the principles of gauging, but, in other refpects, was
altogether untinctured with human learning, and

E 6   fion,

but lately introduced to any fort of decent commerce. The doctor enjoyed a reputable profeffion, a patrimony of five thoufand pounds, and an
extenfive family-intereft; the officer had ten
pounds in his pocket, was one hundred and fifty
in debt to his taylor, and enjoyed a lieutenant's
commiffion; which, by the bye, he owed to the
intereft of the phyfician's father. The doctor
wore a fair perriwig, and a plain fuit of clothes;
the officer his own hair in a bag, an embroidered
coat, a cockade in his hat, and ftone-buckles in
his fhoes; and thefe were the particulars that, in
the lady's opinion, eclipfed all the qualities of the
phyfician. I fhall conclude this comparifon with
obferving, that the doctor, had he been fo minded,
could at any time have rivalled the officer, both
in his finery and rank in the fervice; but it was by
no means in the lieutenant's power to attain the
merit and real importance of the phyfician.

E S S A Y VII.

WHETHER the inftinct of brutes be a fubordinate fpecies of reafon, or an innate faculty imprefled by nature for the prefervation of the individual, is a queftion which has been long contefted among philofophers. That reafon and inftinct are effentially different, appears from the following confiderations : reafon is the refult of ideas acquired, and muft be improved by exercife and cultivation. The inftinct of brutes feems perfect as foon as the animal is produced ; the chick, by a furprifing inftinct, picks a way for itfelf through the fhell into the world, and begins to feed immediately, before it can poffibly have received any ideas from obfervation. The fame faculty is obfervable in blind puppies, and all quadrupeds, which curioufly fearch for the dug in order to fuck the mother. Throw one of thefe blind puppies into a pond of water, and it will fwim with amazing dexterity. This is likewife the cafe with all aquatic fowls, from the moment

they

they are hatched ; and all the birds of the air naturally fly without being inftructed.   All animals,
without prefcription, choofe that kind of food
which nature has allotted them, and, in the exercife of this choice, carefully avoid thofe things
which would prejudice their health, even when
they feem to be folicited by their fenfes : for example, a hog will greedily devour an apple ; but
by no means will touch the fruit of the manza-
nillo tree, which is poifonous, although it refembles an apple in colour, fhape, and odour.   One
beaft, as if it knew by intuition the ftrength of its
own organs, or the peculiarity of their conftruc-
tion, fhall eat and digeft thofe herbs which would
prove fatal to the other animals that graze upon
the fame common.. Nay, if we may believe the
hiftory of medicine, the virtues of many fimples
have been difcovered to mankind by the beafts of
the field, which, from the fame principle, had re-
courfe to their efficacy, when difordered by accident or diftemper.   Among other inftances of inftinct we ought alfo to mention the Στοργη, or natural affection, though it is common to the human fpecies as well as to brutes.   That this is inftinct, totally different from reafon, we may conclude from the different effects it produces in human creatures, and among the brute creation.
The Στοργη of a beaft ceafes from the very inftant
that

that it becomes unneceffary to the prefervation of
the young offspring; and among birds is fucceeded by fuch averfion and animofity in the breaft
of the mother, that fhe commonly drives her progeny into immediate exile : this feems to be the
admirable difpofition of Providence, that one particular place may not be overftocked, and animals
of the fame fpecies diftrefs one another by creat-
ing a fcarcity.

In the human fpecies the Στοργη is protracted
and improved into the charities, by intercourfe and
continuation of good offices, and the exercife of
reafon ; and this in proportion to the ftrength of
reflection and the delicacy of fentiment.   The
lefs enlightened the mother happens to be by human underftanding, the more fhe conforms to this
blind inftinct : an ideot fondled her own child with
all the care, tendernefs, and fkill, which the Στοργη
feems to infpire in the brute animal, till it could
fubfift without the mother's milk, then refigned all
affection and attention to it, and no longer diftinguifhed it as her own offspring.   Obferve the
lower clafs among the vulgar, who, in point of fentiment, are but one degree raifed above the level of
the beafts, with what eagernefs, and even rapture
of affection, a mother will carefs her bantling :
behold the fame mother and the fame child two

or

or three years after, the Στοργὴ is entirely vanished; she looks upon the child as a troublesome incumbrance laid upon her by the law: she fairly
wishes it at the devil, beats it with the utmost
barbarity, and, instead of being the pledge of her
love, it becomes the object of her execration. The
case is no more than this: natural instinct vanished at its usual period, and there was no sentiment
to take its place.

But in nothing does instinct appear more
amazing, than in those curious nests so judi-
ciously contrived, and so wonderfully executed.
by the birds, as receptacles for their young.
It has been often observed, that in this respect they
not only surpass all human art, but defy all imitation. It may also be remarked, that the nest
constructed by any bird in the first year of its ex-
istence, is as uniform and perfect as those which
are built after many years experience. This is,
another strong reason for supposing that instinct
neither depends upon ideas acquired, nor improves
by exercise and observation; consequently, is a
power or faculty altogether distinct from reason,
which is undoubtedly acquired from observation
and extended by practice. It may be asked then,
If the instinct of brutes is produced with the animal in full perfection, how come they to exhibit
such evident marks of docility? Many animals
have

have given proofs of uncommon fagacity, and may be taught a thoufand things that denote a confiderable fhare of reafon. Without all doubt, as the human fpecies have fome kinds of inftinct in common with brutes, fo the brute creation fhare with man a weaker faculty of reafon; but this we conceive to be altogether different from inftinct. Reafon is the power of arranging, comparing, and judging from ideas received; inftinct feems to be a principle previous to all ideas, and independent of them, implanted among the firft ftamina of life. Reafon does not appear till a confiderable time after the animal is born, then fhoots forth like a tender plant, continues to grow, and as it grows acquires frefh vigour from proper cultivation; on the contrary, inftinct appears at once in full maturity. The range of reafon is unbounded, comprehending all arts and all arguments; inftinct is confined to a few articles relating to the prefervation and propagation of the individual. Reafon is fubject to miftake and deception; inftinct is fure and infallible. Man is in fome cafes guided by inftinct, and brutes are fometimes conducted by the faint glimmerings of reafon. A thoufand wonderful inftances are recorded of the fagacity of the elephant, the ingenuity of the ape, the cunning of the fox, and the docility of the dog. We ourfelves could produce

fome

fome furprifing evidence in favour of the afs, which lies (in our opinion unjuftly) under the general reproach of ftupidity ; but as we have not room to infert a number of particulars relating to this fubject, we fhall content ourfelves, and we hope our readers, with one furprizing inftance of refentment and reflection in a ftork, extracted from the Travels of Keyfler.

· "How far a rational principle, mutual affection, and comparifon of ideas, may be afcribed to animals, I will not at prefent determine ; but affure you, that the following adventure of a tame ftork, fome years ago in the Univerfity of Tubingen, is literally true : This bird lived quietly in the court-yard, till Count Victor Gravenitz, then a ftudent there, fhot with ball at a ftork's neft adjacent to the college, and probably wounded the ftork then in it, as he was obferved for fome weeks not to ftir out of the neft. This happened in autumn, when foreign ftorks begin their periodical emigrations. In the enfuing fpring, a ftork was obferved on the roof of the college, and by its inceffant chattering gave the tame ftork, walking below in the area, to underftand, that it would be glad of its company. But this was a thing impracticable, on account of its wings being clipt ; which induced the ftranger with the

the utmoſt precaution firſt to come down to the
upper gallery, the next day ſomething lower, and
at laſt, after a great deal of ceremony, quite into
the court. The tame ſtork, which was con-
ſcious of no harm, went to meet him with a ſoft
cheerful note, and a ſincere intention of giving
him a friendly reception, when, to his great ſur-
prize, the other fell upon him with the utmoſt
fury. The ſpectators preſent, indeed, for that
time, drove away the foreign ſtork ; but this was
ſo far from intimidating him, that he came again
the next day to the charge, and during the whole
ſummer, continual ſkirmiſhes were interchanged
between them. Mr. G. R. v. F. had givenor-
ders that the tame ſtork ſhould not be aſſiſted, as
having only a ſingle antagoniſt to encounter : and
by being thus obliged to ſhift for himſelf, he came
to ſtand better on his guard, and make ſuch a
gallant defence, that at the end of the campaign
the ſtranger had no great advantage to boaſt of.
But next ſpring, inſtead of a ſingle ſtork came
four, which, without any of the foregoing ceremonies, alighted at once in the college area, and
directly attacked the tame ſtork, who, indeed, in
the view of ſeveral ſpectators ſtanding in the gal-
leries, performed feats even above human valour,
if I may uſe that expreſſion, defending himſelf by
the arms Nature had given him, with the utmoſt
bravery,

bravery, till at length, being overpowered by fuperior numbers, his ftrength and courage began to
fail, when very unexpected auxiliaries came in
to his affiftance ; all the turkies, ducks, geefe,
and the reft of the fowls that were brought up in
the court, to whom, undoubtedly, this gentle ftork's mild and friendly behaviour had en-
deared him, without the leaft dread of the danger, formed a kind of rampart round him, under the fhelter of which. he might make an honourable retreat from fo unequal an encounter :
and even a peacock, which before never could
live in friendfhip with him, on this emergency
took the part of oppreffed innocence, and was,
if not a true-bottomed friend, at leaft a favourable
judge on the ftork's fide.

" UPON this, a ftricter watch was kept againft
fuch traitorous incurfions of the enemy, and a
ftop put to more bloodfhed ; till at laft, about
the beginning of the third fpring, above twenty
ftorks alighted in the court with the greateft fury;
and before the poor ftork's faithful life-guards
could form themfelves, or any of the people come
in to his affiftance, they deprived him of life,
though, by exerting his ufual gallantry, they paid
dear for the purchafe.

THE

" The malevolence of thefe ftrangers againft this innocent creature could proceed from no other motive than the fhot fired by Count Victor from the college, and which they doubtlefs fufpected was done by the inftigation of the tame ftork."

ESSAY

E S S A Y VIII.

INQUIRING with myſelf wherein true beauty conſiſts, and how it may be attained, the beſt account I could find for it was true virtue. I know this will appear ſtrange to ſome, but I am not here to enter into metaphyſical diſputes or criticiſms on other people ; I appeal to nature, and ſhall proceed to deliver my opinion.

WHEN all the faculties of the ſoul harmoniouſly conſpire in their ſeveral operations in due proportion to their nature, without jarring and interrupting one another, then the mind is ſerene, and the perſon is virtuous and happy. The outward form, like an inſtrument tuned in concord, preſents to the eye an image of this internal harmony. The face never is a falſe glaſs, but through artifice and bad habits.

WHAT is it in external forms that excites in us the idea of beauty, but the harmony and delicate proportions obſerved in the arrangement of certain

tain

tain particles of matter? But as the foul arranges and moves all matter, thofe harmonies and deli-cacies of proportion never could take place under the influence of an unharmonious mind.

How amiable are the characters of children? and there are few of them come fo far of age, as to have their features diftinctly marked, but who appear pretty; and yet, gradually as they grow up, we often fee their mufcles convulfed by paffions, their features turn coarfer and ftronger, and then their beauty flies.

THERE is a great deal of beauty owing to the happinefs of birth: as for example, where the fa-ther and mother have been well afforted, and lived a temperate life in peace and mutual love; in fuch a cafe, the children are frefh and vigorous, yet the flow of their blood and animal fpirits is not irre-gular; they naturally are more difpofed to a life of tranquillity and virtue, which as it does not ruffle the mind, the face, its image, is more ferene.

I WOULD make allowances for the fmall-pox and other accidents of ficknefs, or the cares and dif-treffes of life that imprint themfelves upon the face. Some of thefe rather confirm than contra-dict our theory; and at any rate they are like
whirlwinds,

whirlwinds, inundations, earthquakes, and other
extraordinary calamities, againſt which no proviſion can be made in the ordinary courſe of human
affairs.   There are, however, many diſtreſſes
which impair beauty, for which people have themſelves to blame, ſuch as the hyſteric diſeaſe. This
indeed chiefly ariſes from ſome unfortunate accident or ſhock to the tender female conſtitution;
but frequently alſo from ſloth and idleneſs, and a
romantic imagination, where there has been no
uſeful buſineſs to keep the mind employed, and proper exerciſe for the health of the body. The laws
of nature are inflexible, the tranſgreſſion of them
always proves its own puniſhment.

READING books of extravagant poetry raiſes
correſponding tumults in the mind, as they paint
all the paſſions immoderate. Tragedies ſuch as
they frequently are, books of romantic love, and,
which is fifty times worſe, books of romantic in-
trigues, all tend to diſturb the breaſt of the tender fair-one. As their imaginations are more
lively than ours, they are more apt to receive
wrong impreſſions, and have their taſte corrupted.
Thus the unfortunate maid pines inwardly from a
wounded imagination, and her corroded beauty
falls a victim to her folly.

                                        IT

" THE malevolence of thefe ftrangers againft this innocent creature could proceed from no other motive that the fhot fired by Count Victor from the college, and which they doubtlefs fufpected was done by the inftigation of the tame ftork."

E S S A Y   VIII.

HOWEVER vain and ridiculous the pre-
sumption of thofe people may appear, who
pretend to tell fortunes, and prognofticate future
events, from the arrangement of cards, and the
appearance of coffee-grounds as they are whirled
around and fettled on the fides of the cup; we
will not fcruple to affirm, that the genuine art of
Phifiognomy, or Metopofcopy, is not beneath
the confideration and even the ftudy of a philofopher : for though it will not teach us to prognofticate particular events, it muft be of confiderable fervice in helping us to difcern the predominant paffions, the vices, the views, and, in
a word, the natural difpofition of thofe with whom
we may have connexions and concerns. This
inference we draw from a thorough conviction,
that the looks of men in general are ftrongly
affected, and even modelled, by particular habits
of thinking; and that different characters of the
mind are ufually diftinguifhed by peculiar con-

formations

formations and complexions of the body. A fub-
tle Italian politician, famous for difcovering the
hidden fentiments of the heart, even when wrap-
ped in the thickeft cloak of diffimulation, ufed
carefully to furvey the features of the perfon whofe
thoughts he wanted to develope, and mimic their
difpofition in his own face; an expedient that
never failed to fuggeft the ideas which correfponded with that caft of countenance. Every-
body has heard the inftance of the phifiognomift
Zopyrus, who having examined the face of
Socrates, pronounced him a dunce and a liber-
tine. This artift being ridiculed by thofe who
were well acquainted with this fage's wifdom and
continence, Socrates reprehended them for their
mirth, and owned he was naturally fuch as the phifiognomift had declared, but that he had corrected
the vices of his nature by the exercife of reafon
and hard ftudy. Another profeffor of metopofcopy having viewed a portrait of Hippocrates,
pronounced nearly the fame fentence againft that
father of medicine, and was in danger of being
roughly handled by his difciples, until they were
undeceived by their mafter, who alfo had candour enough to acknowledge his own natural defects. Pliny, in mentioning the excellency of
the painter Apelles, affirms, that he ftruck the
likenefs of men fo exactly, that a phifiognomift,

F 2   by

by looking at them, could difcover the age of
the perfons reprefented, and even predict the
number of years they had to live. John, fir-
named the FEARLESS, Duke of Burgundy,
being taken prifoner in the battle of Nicopolis,
fought between the Imperialifts and the Turks,
was upon the brink of being put to death, by
order of the victor Sultan Bajazet, when a Turkifh
phifiognomift faved his life, by affuring the Sultan, that from an accurate infpection of the prifoner, he could plainly perceive, that if John was
difmiffed, he would occafion a vaft effufion of
blood and many cruel wars among the Chriftians.
This prediction, however, we muft receive with
fome grains of allowance, though related as a
fact by Henterus in his Hiftory of Burgundy.
We are told by Paulus Jovius, that Antonio
Tiberto, a native of Cefena, and a very famous
phifiognomift, prognofticated to Guido Balneo,
the great favourite of Pandulfo Malatefta, a tyrant
of Arimini, that he would be deprived of life by
an intimate friend of his own. He likewife
warned Pandulpho, that he would be expelled
from his country, and die in extreme mifery.
Both events happened according to the prediction ;
Guido was put to death by the tyrant, who, in his
turn, died in exile, wretchedly poor, and abandoned by all the world. St. Gregory of Nazi-
anzen,

anzen, feeing Julian the Apoftate, when he was a young man, at Athens; after having attentively viewed his face and appearance, exc'aimed, " O what mifchief will that youth occafion to the Roman empire!" St. Charles of Borcmeo paid fuch regard to the phifiognomy, that he would admit none into his family and fervice but perfons of unblemifhed make and agreeable afpect, faying, " that beautiful fouls generally dwelt in beautiful bodies." This general rule, however, is not without numerous exceptions. The Jefuit NICETUS being reputed the beft phifiognomift who hath committed his rules to writing, we fhall fpecify fome of them, for the entertainment of the curious; and every reader may compare them with the refult of his own obfervations.

" A MAN of a *fanguine* or *gay difpofition* is diftinguifhed by a fair fmooth fkin, large mufcles, quick growth, agility, plentiful fweats, a florid complexion, red hair, pleafing afpect, regular features, a ftrong clear and agreeable tone of voice, a ftrong full pulfe, found and long fleeping, pleafing dreams of dancing, riding, or flying. His conftitution is hot and moift; his health various; his life long. His virtues confift in meeknefs, affability, gratitude, and urbanity:

F 3   the

the vices incident to this difpofition are, loquacity, ficklenefs, breach of faith, lying, luft, and
inconftancy. In point of genius, he is volatile,
capricious, and averfe to ftudy.

" THE *choleric* or *fiery difpofition* is known
by a lean habit, agility, a rigid fibre, dufky fkin,
fhort curled hair, fmall head, little eyes, quick
pace, rough tongue, fcanty fecretion of fpittle, a
brown yellowifh complexion, a quick hafty voice,
a vehement hard frequent pulfe, fhort and interrupted fleep, turbulent dreams of wars and quar-
rels. His conftitution is hot and dry, his health
good, and life of a reafonable length. His virtues confift in diligence, ftrength, vigilance, and
conftancy. With refpect to vices, he is irafcible,
quarrelfome, apt to indulge hatred, ambitious,
boaftful, importunate, impolite, and invidious.
His genius is keen, penetrating, and fagacious.

" THE *phlegmatic difpofition* is attended with
bulk, fullnefs, a great deal of fpittle and mucus
but no drought, grey hairs betimes, fmall blood-
veffels, flow digeftion, a white jolly fleek effe-
minate countenance, a fharp quick fqueaking
voice, a flow deliberate equal pulfe, fweet eafy
long fleeps ; dreams of water, or moift objects.
His conftitution is cold and moift, his health in-
different,

different, and life fhort. In point of virtue, he is meek, quiet, and inoffenfive in converfation. As to vice, he is idle, flothful, luxurious, and impolite; and with refpect to genius, he is dull, and flow of comprehenfion.

" HE that inherits a *melancholic* or *terrene difpofition* has a fmall body, beardlefs thin dry rough fkin, and hard bones, a grey dufky leaden dejected countenance, a low quivering fearful voice, a flow fmall hard pulfe, troubled fleep, melancholy dreams of the dead. His conftitution is cold and dry, his health very bad, and his life of fhort duration. The virtues of this difpofition are, fidelity, ftability, and prudence; but this more remarkable in youth than in old age. The vices are, fullen filence, avarice, obftinacy, and a fufpicious temper. The genius is profound, perfevering, and mature.

" STRENGTH OF BODY is known by ftiff hair, large bones, fwelling firm and robuft limbs, fhort mufcular neck, firm and erect; the hind-headbroad and high, the fore-head fhort hard and pecked, with briftly hair; large feet, rather thick than broad; a harfh unequal voice, and choleric complexion.

" WEAK-

" WEAKNESS OF BODY is diftinguifhed by a fmall ill-proportioned head, narrow fhoulders, foft fkin, and melancholy complexion.

" THE figns of *long life* are, ftrong teeth, a fan-guine temperament, middle ftature, large deep and ruddy lines in the hand, large mufcles, ftoop-ing fhoulders, full cheft, firm flefh, clear com-plexion, flow growth, wide ears, large eyelids, and the hollow of the navel equally wide at top and bottom.

" SHORT LIFE may be inferred from a thick tongue, the appearance of grinders before the age of puberty, thin ftraggling and uneven teeth, con-fufed lines in the hand, quick but fmall growth, the lower part of the navel wider than the brim, and a melancholy temperament.

" A GOOD GENIUS may be expected from a thin fkin, middling ftature, blue light eyes, fair com-plexion, ftraight and pretty ftrong hair, large hands and fingers, an affable afpect, the eye-brows joined, moderation in mirth, an open front, the temples a little concave, and the head fhaped like a mallet.

" A DUNCE may be known by a fwoln neck, plump arms fides and loins, a round head concave behind,

behind, a large flefhy forehead, pale eyes, dead heavy look, fmall joints, fnuffling noftrils, prick-ears, pronenefs to laughter, little hands, an ill-protioned head, either too big or too little, blubber lips, fhort fingers, and thick legs.

" FORTITUDE may be guefled from a wide mouth, a fonorous voice, grave flow and always equal, upright pofture, large eyes, pretty open and ftedfaft, the hair high above the forehead, the head pretty much compreffed or flattened, the forehead fquare and high, the extremities large and robuft, the neck firm, though not flefhy, a large corpulent cheft, and brown complexion.

" BOLDNESS is characterifed by a prominent mouth, rugged appearance, rough forehead, arched eye-brows, large noftrils and teeth, fhort neck, big arms, ample cheft, fquare fhoulders, and froward afpect.

" PRUDENCE is generally diftinguifhed by an head flat on the fides, a broad fquare forehead, a little concave in the middle, a foft voice, large cheft, thin hair, large eyes, either blue brown or black, pretty large ears, and an aquiline nofe.

" A GOOD MEMORY is commonly attached to thofe perfons who are fmaller, yet better formed in

the

upper than in the lower parts, not fat but flefhy, of
a fair delicate fkin, with the poll of the head unco-
vered, crooked nofe, teeth thick fet, large ears,
with plenty of cartilage.

"A BAD MEMORY is obfervable in perfons who
are larger in their fuperior than inferior parts,
flefhy, though dry and bald. *N. B.* This is exprefly
contrary to the remark of Ariftotle, who fays,
that the fuperior parts being larger than the inferior fignify a good memory, and *vice verfâ.*

" A GOOD IMAGINATION *and thoughtful difpofition* is diftinguifhed by a large prominent forehead, a fixed and attentive look, flow refpiration,
and an inclination of the head.

"PERSONS who enjoy a *good fight* have generally
black thick ftraight eye-lafhes, large bufhy
eye-brows, concave eyes, contracted as it were
inwards.

" SHORT-SIGHTED PEOPLE have a ftern or ear-
neft look, fmall fhort eye brows, large pupils, and
prominent eyes.

"THOSE who poffefs *the fenfe of hearing* in perfection, have ears well furnifhed with griftle, well
channelled, and hairy.

" THE

" The *sense of smelling* is most perfect in those who have large noses, descending very near the mouth, neither too moist nor too dry.

" A nice *faculty of tasting* is peculiar to such as have a spongy porous soft tongue, well moistened with saliva, yet not too moist.

" Delicacy *in the touch* belongs to those who have a soft skin, sensible nerves, and nervous sinews moderately warm and dry.

" Irascibility is accompanied by an erect posture, a clear skin, solemn voice, open nostrils, moist temples displaying superficial veins, thick neck, equal use of both hands, quick pace, bloodshot eyes, large unequal ill-ranged teeth, and choleric complexion.

" Timorousness resides where we find a concave nape of the neck, pale colour, weak winking eyes, soft hair, long slender neck, smooth plump breast, shrill tremulous voice, small round mouth, thin lips, broad thin hands, and small shambling feet.

" Melancholy is denoted by a wrinkled front, dejected eyes, meeting eye-brows, slow pace, fixed look, and deliberate respiration.

F 6   " An

" An *amorous difpofition* may be known by a fair flender face, a redundancy of hair, rough temples, broad forehead, gracious look, moift fhining eyes, wide noftrils, narrow fhoulders, hairy hands and arms, legs well fhaped and finewy.

" GAIETY attends a ferene open forehead, rofy agreeable countenance, a fweet mufical tone of voice, an agile body, and foft flefh.

" ENVY appears with a wrinkled forehead, frowning dejected and fquinting look, a pale melancholy afpect, a dry rough fkin, and hard bones.

" INTREPIDITY often refides in a fmall body, with red curled hair, ruddy countenance, fquare forehead, frowning eye-brows arched and meeting, rolling eyes, blue or yellowifh, a large mouth, and reddifh lines in the palm of the hand.

" GENTLENESS, *or complacency*, may be diftinguifhed by a foft and moift palm, frequency of fhutting the eyes, foft movement, flow fpeech, foft ftraight and red hair.

" BASHFULNESS may be difcovered by moift eyes, never wide open, eye-brows frequently lowered, blufhing cheeks, moderate pace, flow and

and fubmiffive fpeech, bent body, and glowing ears of a purple hue.

" TEMPERANCE, *or fobriety,* is accompanied with an equal refpiration, a moderate fized mouth, fmooth temples, eyes of an ordinary fize, either fair or azure, and a fhort flat belly,

" STRENGTH *of mind* is fignified by red curled hair, a fmall body, fhining eyes, but a little de-preffed, a grave intenfe voice, bufhy beard, large broad back and fhoulders.

" PRIDE ftands confeffed with arched eye-brows, large prominent mouth, a broad cheft, flow pace, erected head, fhrugging fhoulders, and ftaring eyes.

" LUXURY dwells with a ruddy or palifh com-plexion, downy temples, bald pate, little eyes, thick neck, corpulent body, large nofe, ftrutting belly, thin eye-brows, and hands covered with a kind of down.

" LOQUACITY may be expected from a bufhy beard, broad fingers, pointed tongue, eyes of a ruddy hue, a large prominent upper lip, a downy belly, and fharp-pointed nofe.

" PERVERSE-

" PERVERSENESS may be dreaded when we perceive a high forehead, firm fhort thick im-
moveable neck, quick fpeech, immoderate laughter, fiery eyes, fhort flefhy hands and fingers.

" IMPUDENCE may be inferred from fiery
ftaring eyes, eager look, circular forehead, round
ruddy countenance, elevated cheft, flat nofe, and
loud laughter."

ESSAY

E S S A Y   IX.

OF all vulgar errors and idle remarks, that of Fafcination, or the Evil Eye, is the moft common, and perhaps the moft ancient. This fpecies of fuperftition generally prevailed among the Romans, as we learn from the teftimony of Pliny, Plutarch, Aulus Gellius, and others, not forgetting the hackneyed line of Virgil,

Nefcio quis teneros oculus mihi fafcinat agnos.

PLUTARCH, who beftows a dialogue exprefsly on this fubject, gives us to underftand, that the conceit of Fafcination was derived from the moft remote antiquity. In Greece it was common in the time of Ariftotle, who obferves in one of his problems, that the herb rue was accounted a fpecific againft Fafcination. To the prepoffeffion of fo many ages, we may add the fuffrage of many learned men, theologifts as well as phyficians.

FOR thefe reafons, a man at firft fight who barely follows the rules of common criticifm, would

would believe that Fafcination really exifted, and
even look upon it as a flagrant piece of rafh
prefumption to deny that which at all times
hath been adopted by the common confent of
all nations: but we, who know the facility with
which a falfe opinion is communicated from one
perfon to another, and laugh at the common
notions of the multitude, poffefs, thank heaven! a
mind quite free from either the fear or veneration,
which the opinions of the vulgar ufually infpire,
and altogether unreftrained by the authority of
ages, or the confent of nations. On the contrary, we are perfuaded that the whole doctrine
of Fafcination is a mere fable, produced and nou-
rifhed among ignorant, rude, and fuperftitious
people, and afterwards communicated through
want of reflection to perfons of greater capacity.

FASCINATION is fuppofed to be the action of
injuring any perfon by a glance of the eye; but
it is commonly imagined, as a neceffary circumftance, that the fafcinator muft look at the perfon fafcinated with an emotion of envy. Beautiful children are thought to be the moft expofed
to this damage, becaufe the tendernefs of their
conftitution is more capable of receiving a ma-
lignant impreffion, and their beauty excites the
                                                    envy

'envy of the beholders. Some fuppofe, that not only envy, but likewife love fometimes produces the fame effect, which is likewife occafioned by praifing as well as by looking upon the object.

PLAIN and obvious it is, that according to found philofophy, neither the one nor the other can make the leaft impreffion. The eye-fight is not active, but confined within its proper organ, which receives the pictures from the object, but fends nothing to it in return: neither do words, either of praife or difparagement, poffefs any phyfical power of action, having nothing but the fignification or intentional reprefentation which hath been affixed to them by the arbitrary will of mankind; therefore all that has been faid of Fafcination is a mere chimæra.

AMONG the medical authors who treat of this fubject, Vallis fufpects that the error arifes from this circumftance: That handfome, healthy, and flefhy children are the moft fubject to be feized with fome dangerous indifpofition; in confirmation of which he quotes an aphorifm from Hippocrates: *Habitus, qui ad fummum boni-tatis pertingit, periculofus eft*; and that of Cornelius Celfus: *Qui nitidiores folito funt, fufpecta bona,*

bona, fua habere debent. " Now (fays he)
the vulgar being ignorant of this rule in medicine, or this law of nature, impute the fuddcn
tranfition from health to ficknefs in fuch childrcn,
to the evil eye of thofe who look upon them."
Whether thefe two aphorifms be true or falfe,
certain it is they are here mifapplied by Vallis ;
firft, becaufe neither Hippocrates nor Celfus fays
that, in this ftate of perfect health, the tranfition
to diftemper is fudden ; and fecondly, becaufe
both are equally applicable to adults and children, and thus are generally underftood by phyficians. Nor, in fact, do we believe that this fudden
failure of health in children is frequent : if it happens oftener in them than in adults, it ought to
be attributed to the tendernefs and little ftrength
of the fibres, which, being incapable of making
much refiftance, may, from various caufes, internal as well as external, fuddenly lofe their
tone. This, no doubt, is the moft probable
caufe of thofe fudden changes ; whereas that of
the influence of evil eyes is totally improbable,
not only for the reafons we have already given,
but alfo for this we are going to add.

WERE the common notion true, thofe children
would be the moft frequently fafcinated who are
moft likely to excite envy ; I mean the children of
noblemen

noblemen and opulent perfons, who generally appear the moſt neat, jolly, clean, handſome, and
richly clothed : whereas the contrary is evident ;
for thoſe who moſt generally complain of their
children being bewitched, are poor low creatures.
Indeed the caſe is very plain.   As they take leſs
care of them, and frequently expoſe them to the
weather, to extreme cold, and exceſſive heat, as
well as many other inconveniences, they muſt of
courſe be more ſubject to thoſe ſudden accidents.
Nevertheleſs, with reſpect to the children of the
gentry, other cauſes may give riſe to this ſuperſti-
tious belief. We have heard of a lady, who, in her
childhood, never went to church without being
taken with ſome diſorder. The reaſon was, that, in
dreſſing her for the occaſion, they tied her garments ſo ſtrait as to impede the circulation of the
blood. This cauſe, in a little time, produced
the indiſpoſition we have mentioned ; the reaſon
of which ſhe very well knew, and did not fail to
lament : but it could never be driven out of the
heads of the ſervants, that when ſhe appeared in
public, with the additional circumſtances of beauty
and rich apparel, ſhe always ſuffered by an evil
eye.

We cannot help obſerving, that the common
precaution taken againſt an evil eye, by hanging
round

round the necks of children a little hand made of jet, or other figure, fignifying derifion and contempt, in order to defend them from the evil influence of envious eyes, is inherited by lawful fucceffion from the fuperftition of the Gentiles.

AMONG the multitude of ridiculous deities which the Romans adored, there was one called FASCINO, upon whom they conferred that name, becaufe they believed him capable of protecting perfons from the power of Fafcination. The image of this divinity, who was exceffively ugly and extremely ridiculous, they not only hung to the necks of their infants, but even fixed to their triumphal chariots ; perfuaded that thofe who appeared in all the glory of a triumph, were, as objects of the moft rancorous envy, under the neceffity of having fome fuch protection. The conformity of the rites fhews, that the cuftom of thefe days took its origin from the practice of antiquity.

THE argument which the patrons of Fafcination ufe in favour of this opinion, by alledging the fteams or noxious effluvia which proceed from fome bodies, is of no weight nor confequence to the fubject : firft, becaufe the motion of thefe effluvia does not depend upon the fenfe of feeing ; for he that is poffeffed of thefe effluvia will not

fail

fail to fend them forth, whether he does or does not look upon any object : fecondly, becaufe the courfe of them does not depend upon the affection of envy, or of love ; but folely on the internal or external heat by which they are agitated, and exhaled from the body. It may be faid, perhaps, that there is one particular kind of poifonous effluvia, which flows from the eyes only : but this is a new fyftem of phyfics, invented at pleafure, for no other purpofe than to fupport the other fable. But, granting that the pores of the eyes are the only conduits for thefe effluvia, as foon as they come forth, they muft be difperfed in the circumambient air, like all other effluvia, inftead of going in a ftraight line to the object of view. The action of looking can never direct them to the object, becaufe, as we have already hinted, that action is immanent, to ufe the terms of philofophy : in other words, it has no effect outwards; but is wholly exerted within the organ of fight.

WITH refpect to the other argument, founded on various examples of birds being killed, and mirrors broken, merely by being looked upon by thofe who poffefs this inherent venom, we fhall anfwer them in the words of Vallis, *meræ nugæ, meræ fabulæ.*

ESSAY

E S S A Y X.

I TAKE the liberty to communicate to the public, a few loose thoughts upon a subject, which, though often handled, has not yet, in my opinion, been fully discussed: I mean National Concord, or Unanimity, which, in this kingdom, has been generally considered as a bare possibility, that existed nowhere but in speculation. Such an union is, perhaps, neither to be expected nor wished for, in a country whose liberty depends rather upon the genius of the people, than upon any precautions which they have taken in a conftitutional way for the guard and preservation of this inestimable blessing.

THERE is a very honest gentleman with whom I have been acquainted these thirty years, during which there has not been one speech uttered against the Ministry in parliament, nor a struggle at an election for a burgess to serve in the House of Commons, nor a pamphlet published in opposition to any measure of the Administration, nor

even

even a private cenfure paffed in his hearing upon
the mifconduct of any perfon concerned in public
affairs, but he is immediately alarmed, and loudly
exclaims againft fuch factious doings, in order to
fet the people by the ears together at fuch a delicate juncture. "At any other time (fays he)
fuch oppofition might not be improper, and I don't
queftion the facts that are alledged; but at this
crifis, Sir, to inflame the nation!—the man de-
ferves to be punifhed as a traitor to his country."
In a word, according to this Gentleman's opinion,
the nation has been in a violent crifis at any time
thefe thirty years; and were it poffible for him to
live another centurv, he would never find any period at which a man might with fafety impugn the
infallibility of a Minifter.

THE cafe is no more than this: My honeft
friend has invefted his whole fortune in the Stocks,
on Government fecurity, and trembles at every
whiff of popular difcontent. Were every Britifh
fubject of the fame tame and timid difpofition,
Magna Charta (to ufe the coarfe phrafe of Oliver
Cromwell) would be no more regarded by an ambitious Prince than Magna F—ta, and the Liberties of England expire without a groan. Oppofition, when reftrained within due bounds, is the
falubrious gale that ventilates the opinions of the
people,

people, which might otherwife ftagnate into the·
moft abject fubmiffion. It may be faid to purify
the atmofphere of politics ; to difpel the grofs
vapours raifed by the influence of Minifterial artifice and corruption, until the Conftitution, like
a mighty rock, ftands full difclofed to the view
of every individual who dwells within the fhade
of its protection. Even when this gale blows
with augmented violence, it generally tends to the
advantage of the Commonwealth : it awakes the
apprehenfion, and confequently aroufes all the faculties of the pilot at the helm, who redoubles his
vigilance and caution, exerts his utmoft fkill, and,
becoming acquainted with the nature of the navi-
gation, in a little time learns to fuit his canvafs to
the roughnefs of the fea, and the trim of the veffel. Without thefe intervening ftorms of Oppofition to exercife his faculties, he would become
enervate,   negligent,   and prefumptuous ; and,
in the wantonnefs of his power, trufting to fome
deceitful calm, perhaps hazard a ftep that would
wreck the Conftitution. Yet there is a meafure
in all things. A moderate froft will fertilize the
glebe with nitrous particles, and deftroy the eggs
of pernicious infects, that prey upon the fancy of
the year : but if this froft increafes in feverity and
duration, it will chill the feeds, and even freeze
up the roots of vegetables ; it will check the
bloom,

bloom, nip the buds, and blaft all the promife of the fpring. The vernal breeze that drives the ██████before it, that brufhes the cobwebs from the boughs, that fans the air and fofters vegetation, if augmented to a tempeft, will ftrip the leaves, over-throw the tree, and defolate the garden. The aufpicious gale before which the trim veffel plows the bofom of the fea, while the mariners are kept alert in duty and in fpirits, if converted to a hurricane, overwhelms the crew with terror and confufion. The fails are rent, the cordage cracked, the mafts give way ; the mafter eyes the havock with mute defpair, and the veffel founders in the ftorm. Oppofition, when confined with-in its proper channel, fweeps away thofe beds of foil and banks of fand which corruptive power had gathered ; but when it overflows its banks, and deluges the plain, its courfe is marked by ruin and devaftation.

THE Oppofition neceffary in a free State like that of Great Britain, is not at all incompatible with that National Concord which ought to unite the people on all emergencies in which the general fafety is at ftake. It is the jealoufy of patriotifm, not the rancour of party ; the warmth of candour, not the virulence of hate ; a tranfient difpute among friends, not an implacable feud, that ad-

VOL. I.   G   mits

mits of no reconciliation. The hiftory of all
ages teems with the fatal effects of internal difcord ; and were hiftory and tradition annihilated,
common fenfe would plainly point out the mif-
chiefs that muft arife from want of harmony and
national union. Every fchool-boy can have re-
courfe to the fable of the rods, which, when
united in a bundle, no ftrength could bend ; but
when feparaed into fingle twigs, a child could
break with eafe.

E S S A Y

E S S A Y XI.

I HAVE fpent the greater part of my life in making obfervations on men and things, and in projecting fchemes for the advantage of my country; and though my labours have met with an ungrateful return, I will ftill perfift in my endeavours for its fervice, like that venerable, unfhaken, and neglected patriot Mr. JACOB HENRI-QUEZ, who, though of the Hebrew nation, hath exhibited a fhining example of Chriftian fortitude and perfeverance*. And here my confcience urges me to confefs, that the hint upon which the following propofals are built, was taken from an advertifement of the faid patriot HENRIQUEZ, in which he gives the public to underftand, that Heaven had indulged him with "feven blcffed

---

* A man well known at this period (1762), as well as during many preceding years, for the numerous fchemes he was daily offering to various Minifters for the purpofe of raifing money by loans, paying off the national incumbrances, &c. &c. none of which, however, were ever known to have received the fmalleft notice.

daugh-

daughters." Bleſſed they are, no doubt, on account
of their own and their father's virtues; but more
bleſſed may they be, if the ſcheme I offer ſhould
be adopted by the Legiſlature.

THE proportion which the number of females
born in theſe kingdoms bears to the male children,
is, I think, ſuppoſed to be as thirteen to four-
teen: but as women are not ſo ſubject as the
other ſex to accidents and intemperance, in numbering adults we ſhall find the balance on the female ſide. If, in calculating the numbers of the
people, we take in the multitudes that emigrate
to the Plantations, from whence they never return, thoſe that die at ſea and make their exit at
Tyburn, together with the conſumption of the
preſent war by ſea and land in the Atlantic, Me-
diterranean, in the German and Indian Oceans,
in Old France, New France, North America,
the Leeward Iſlands, Germany, Africa, and Aſia,
we may fairly ſtate the loſs of men during the war
at one hundred thouſand. If this be the caſe,
there muſt be a ſuperplus of the other ſex amounting to the ſame number, and this ſuperplus will
conſiſt of women able to bear arms; as I take it
for granted, that all thoſe who are fit to bear children are likewiſe fit to bear arms. Now as we
have ſeen the nation governed by old women, I
hope to make appear that it may be defended by

young

young women ; and furely this fcheme will not be rejected as unneceffary at fuch a juncture *, when our armies in the four quarters of the globe are in want of recruits ; when we find ourfelves en-tangled in a new war with Spain, on the eve of a rupture in Italy, and indeed in a fair way of be-ing obliged to make head againft all the great Potentates of Europe.

But, before I unfold my defign, it may be neceffary to obviate, from experience as well as ar-gument, the objections which may be made to the delicate frame and tender difpofition of the female fex rendering them incapable of the toils, and infuperably averfe to the horrors of war. All the world has heard of the nation of Amazons, who inhabited the banks of the river Thermo-doon in Cappadocia ; who expelled their men by force of arms, defended themfelves by their own prowefs, managed the reins of government, pro-fecuted the operations in war, and held the other fex in the utmoft contempt. We are informed by Homer, that Penthefilea, queen of the Ama-zons, acted as auxiliary to Priam, and fell vali-antly fighting in his caufe before the walls of Troy. Quintus Curtius tells us, that Thaleftris brought one hundred armed Amazons in a prefent

* In the year 1762.

G 3

to Alexander the Great. Diodorus Siculus exprefsly fays, there was a nation of female warriors in Africa, who fought againſt the Lybian
Hercules. We read in the Voyages of Colum-
bus, that one of the Caribbee Iſlands was pof-
feſſed by a tribe of female warriors, who kept all
the neighbouring Indians in awe; but we need
not go further than our own age and country to
prove, that the ſpirit and conſtitution of the fair
fex are equal to the dangers and fatigues of war.
Every novice who has read the authentic and im-
portant Hiſtory of the Pirates, is well acquainted
with the exploits of two heroines, called MARY
READ and ANNE BONNY. I myſelf have had the
honour to drink with ANNE CASSIER, alias Mo-
THER WADE, who had diſtinguiſhed herſelf among
the Buccaneers of America, and in her old age kept
a punch-houſe in Port-Royal of Jamaica. I
have likewiſe converſed with MOLL DAVIS, who
had ſerved as a dragoon in all queen Anne's wars,
and was admitted on the penſion of Chelſea.
The late war with Spain, and even the preſent,
hath produced inſtances of females enliſting both
in the land and fea fervice, and behaving with
remarkable bravery in the diſguiſe of the other
fex. And who has not heard of the celebrated
JENNY CAMERON, and ſome other enterpriſing
ladies of North-Britain, who attended a certain
Adven-

Adventurer in all his expeditions, and headed their refpective clans in a military character? That ftrength of body is often equal to the courage of mind implanted in the fair fex, will not be denied by thofe who have feen the water-women of Plymouth; the female drudges of Ireland, Wales, and Scotland; the fifhwomen of Billingfgate; the weeders, podders, and hoppers, who fwarm in the fields; and the bunters who fwagger in the ftreets of London; not to mention the indefatigable trulls who follow the camp, and keep up with the line of march, though loaded with bantlings and other baggage.

THERE is fcarcely a ftreet in this metropolis without one or more viragos, who difcipline their hufbands and domineer over the whole neighbourhood. Many months are not elapfed fince I was witnefs to a pitched battle between two athletic females, who fought with equal fkill and fury until one of them gave out, after having fuftained feven falls on the hard ftones. They were both ftripped to the under-petticoat; their breafts were carefully fwathed with hand-kerchiefs, and as no veftiges of features were to be feen in either when I came up, I imagined the combatants were of the other fex, until a by-

G 4.   ftander

ſtander aſſured me of the contrary, giving me to
underſtand, that the conqueror had lain-in about
five weeks of twin baſtards, begot by her ſecond, who was an Iriſh chairman. When I
ſee the avenues of the Strand beſet every night
with troops of fierce Amazons, who, with dreadful imprecations, ſtop and beat and plunder paſ-
ſengers, I cannot help wiſhing, that ſuch mar-
tial talents were converted to the benefit of the
public ; and that thoſe who are ſo loaded with
temporal fire, and ſo little afraid of eternal fire,
ſhould, inſtead of ruining the ſouls and bodies
of their fellow-citizens, be put in a way of
turning their deſtructive qualities againſt the
enemies of the nation.

HAVING thus demonſtrated that the fair ſex
are not deficient in ſtrength and reſolution, I
would humbly propoſe, that as there is an exceſs on their ſide in quantity to the amount of
one hundred thouſand, part of that number may
be employed in recruiting the army, as well as
in raiſing thirty new Amazonian regiments, to
be commanded by females, and ſerve in regi-
mentals adapted to their ſex. The Amazons
of old appeared with the left breaſt bare, an open
jacket, and trowſers that deſcended no farther
than the knee ; the right breaſt was deſtroyed,

that

that it might not impede them in bending the bow, or darting the javelin ; but there is no occafion for this cruel excifion in the prefent difcipline, as we have feen inftances of women who handle the mufquet, without finding any inconvenience from that protuberance.

As the fex love gaiety, they may be cloathed in vefts of pink fattin and open drawers of the fame, with bufkins on their feet and legs, their hair tied behind and floating on their fhoulders, and their hats adorned with white feathers : they may be armed with light carbines and long bayonets, without the incumbrance of fwords or fhoulder-belts. I make no doubt but many young ladies of figure and fafhion will undertake to raife companies at their own expence, provided they like their colonels ; but I muft infift upon it, if this fcheme fhould be embraced, that Mr. HENRIQUEZ's feven bleffed Daughters may be provided with commiffions, as the project is in fome meafure owing to the hints of that venerable patriot. I moreover give it as my opinion, that Mrs. KITTY FISHER * fhall have the command of a battalion, and the nomination of her own officers, provided fhe will warrant them all found, and be content to wear proper badges of diftinction.

* A celebrated Courtezan of that time.

G 5   A FEMALE

A FEMALE brigade, properly difciplined and accoutred, would not, I am perfuaded, be afraid to charge a numerous body of the enemy, over whom they would have a manifeft advantage; for if the barbarous Scythians were afhamed to fight with the Amazons who invaded them, furely the French, who pique themfelves on their fenfibility and devotion to the fair fex, would not act upon the offenfive againft a band of female warriors, arrayed in all the charms of youth and beauty.

ESSAY

E S S A Y XII.

A S I am one of that fauntering tribe of mortals who fpend the greateft part of their
time in taverns, coffee-houfes, and other places
of public refort, I have thereby an opportunity
of obferving an infinite variety of characters,
which, to a perfon of a contemplative turn, is
a much higher entertainment than a view of all
the curiofities of art or nature. In one of thefe
my late rambles, I accidentally fell into the company of half a dozen gentlemen, who were engaged in a warm difpute about fome political
affair; the decifion of which, as they were equally
divided in their fentiments, they thought proper
to refer to me, which naturally drew me in for a
fhare of the converfation.

AMONGST a multiplicity of other topics, we
took occafion to talk of the different characters
of the feveral nations of Europe; when one of
the gentlemen, cocking his hat, and affuming

fuch

fuch an air of importance as if he had poffeffed all the merit of the Englifh nation in his own per-fon, declared that the Dutch were a parcel of avaricious wretches; the French a fet of flat-tering fycophants; that the Germans were drunken fots, and beaftly gluttons; and the Spaniards proud, haughty, and furly tyrants: but that, in bravery, generofity, clemency, and in every other virtue, the Englifh excelled all the other world.

THIS very *learned* and *judicious remark* was received with a general fmile of approbation by all the company—all, I mean, but your Hum-ble Servant; who, endeavouring to keep my gravity as well as I could, and reclining my head upon my arm, continued for fome time in a pofture of affected thoughtfulnefs, as if I had been mufing on fomething elfe, and did not feem to attend to the fubject of converfation; hoping, by this means, to avoid the difagreeable neceffity of explaining myfelf, and thereby depriving the gentleman of his imaginary happinefs.

BUT my pfeudo-patriot had no mind to let me efcape fo eafily. Not fatisfied that his opinion fhould pafs without contradiction, he was de-termined to have it ratified by the fuffrage of
every

every one in the company; for which purpofe, addreffing himfelf to me with an air of inexpreffible confidence, he afked me if I was not of the fame way of thinking. As I am never forward in giving my opinion, efpecially when I have reafon to believe that it will not be agreeable ; fo, when I am obliged to give it, I always hold it for a maxim to fpeak my real fentiments. I therefore told him, that for my own part, I fhould not have ventured to talk in fuch a peremptory ftrain, unlefs I had made the tour of Europe, and examined the manners of thefe feveral nations with great care and accuracy : that, perhaps, a more impartial judge would not fcruple to affirm, that the Dutch were more frugal and induftrious, the French more temperate and polite, the Germans more hardy and patient of labour and fatigue, and the Spaniards more ftaid and fedate, than the Englifh ; who, though undoubtedly brave and generous, were at the fame time rafh, headftrong, and impetuous ; too apt to be elated with profperity, and to defpond in adverfity.

I could eafily perceive, that all the company began to regard me with a jealous eye before I had finifhed my anfwer, which I had no fooner done, than the patriotic gentleman obferved, with

a con-

a contemptuous fneer, that he was greatly furprized how fome people could have the confcience
to live in a country wh'ch they did not love,
and to enjoy the protection of a government to
which in their hearts they were inveterate enemies. Finding that, by this modeft declaration
of my fentiments, I had forfeited the good opinion of my companions, and given them occafion
to call my political principles in queftion, and
well knowing that it was in vain to argue with
men who were fo very full of themfelves, I
threw down my reckoning, and retired to
my own lodgings, reflecting on the abfurd and
ridiculous nature of national prejudice and prepoffeffion.

AMONG all the famous fayings of antiquity,
there is none that does greater honour to the author, or affords greater pleafure to the reader
(at leaft if he be a perfon of a generous and benevolent heart) than that of the philofopher, who,
being afked what "countryman he was," replied,
that he was "a citizen of the world." How few
are there to be found in modern times who can
fay the fame, or whofe conduct is confiftent with
fuch a profeffion? We are now become fo much
Englifhmen, Frenchmen, Dutchmen, Spaniards,
or Germans, that we are no longer citizens of the
world :

world : fo much the natives of one particular fpot,
or members of one petty fociety, that we no longer confider ourfelves as the general inhabitants of
the globe, or members of that grand fociety which
comprehends the whole human kind.

Dɪᴅ thefe prejudices prevail only among the
meaneft and loweft of the people, perhaps they
might be excufed, as they have few, if any, opportunities of correcting them by reading, travelling,
or converfing with foreigners ; but the misfortune
is, that they infect the minds, and influence the
conduct, even of our gentlemen ; of thofe, I.
mean, who have every title to this appellation but
an exemption from prejudice, which, however, in
my opinion, ought to be regarded as the charac-
teriftical mark of a gentleman ; for let a man's
birth be ever fo high, his ftation ever fo exalted,
or his fortune ever fo large, yet if he is not free
from national and all other prejudices, I fhould
make bold to tell him, that he had a low and vulgar mind, and had no juft claim to the character
of a gentleman. And, in fact, you will always
find, that thofe are moft apt to boaft of national merit, who have little or no merit of their
own to depend on; than which, to be fure, nothing is more natural : the flender vine twifts
around

around the fturdy oak for no other reafon in the
world, but becaufe it has not ftrength fufficient to
fupport itfelf.

SHOULD it be alledged in defence of national
prejudice, that it is the natural and neceffary
growth of love to our country, and that therefore
the former cannot be deftroyed without hurting
the latter, I anfwer, that this is a grofs fallacy
and delufion. That it is the growth of love to our
country, I will allow ; but that it is the natural
and neceffary growth of it, I abfolutely deny. Su-
perftition and enthufiafm too are the growth of
religion ; but who ever took it in his head to affirm, that they are the neceffary growth of this
noble principle ? They are, if you will, the baf-
tard fprouts of this heavenly plant, but not its
natural and genuine branches, and may fafely
enough be lopt off, without doing any harm to the
parent ftock : nay, perhaps, till once they are
lopt off, this goodly tree can never flourifh in perfect health and vigour.

Is it not very poffible that I may love my own
country, without hating the natives of other countries ? that I may exert the moft heroic bravery,
the moft undaunted refolution, in defending its
laws and liberty, without defpifing all the reft of
the

the world as cowards and poltrons ? Moſt certainly
it is ; and if it were not—But what need I ſuppoſe
what is abſolutely impoſſible ?——But if it were
not, I muſt own I ſhould prefer the title of the
ancient philoſopher, *viz.* a Citizen of the World,
to that of an Engliſhman, a Frenchman, an Eu-
ropean, or to any other appellation whatever.

E S S A Y

E S S A Y XIII.

AMIDST the frivolous purſuits and pernicious diſſipations of the preſent age, a reſpect for the qualities of the underſtanding ſtill. prevails to ſuch a degree, that almoſt every individual pretends to have a TASTE for the BELLES LETTRES.. The ſpruce prentice ſets up for a critic, and the. puny beau piques himſelf upon being a connoiſſeur.. Without aſſigning cauſes for this univerſal preſumption, we ſhall proceed to obſerve, that if it was attended with no other inconvenience than that of expoſing the pretender to the ridicule of thoſe few who can ſift his pretenſions, it might be unneceſſary to undeceive the public, or to endeavour at the reformation of innocent folly, productive of no evil to the commonwealth. But in reality this folly is productive of manifold evils to the community. If the reputation of TASTE can be acquired without the leaſt aſſiſtance of literature, by reading modern poems, and ſeeing modern plays, what perſon will deny himſelf the pleaſure.

fure of fuch an eafy qualification ? Hence the youth of both fexes are debauched to diverfion, and feduced from much more profitable occupations into idle endeavours after literary fame; and a fuperficial falfe Tafte, founded on ignorance and conceit, takes poffeffion of the public. The acquifition of learning, the ftudy of nature, is neglected as fuperfluous labour; and the beft faculties of the mind remain unexercifed, and indeed unopened, by the power of thought and reflection. Falfe Tafte will not only diffufe itfelf through all our amufements, but even influence our moral and political conduct : for what is falfe Tafte, but want of perception to difcern propriety and diftinguifh beauty?

IT has been often alledged, that Tafte is a natural talent, as independent of art as ftrong eyes, or a delicate fenfe of fmelling ; and, without all doubt, the principal ingredient in thecompofition of Tafte is a natural fenfibility, without which it cannot exift ; but it differs from the fenfes in this particular, that they are finifhed by nature; whereas Tafte cannot be brought to perfection without proper cultivation: for Tafte pretends to judge not only of nature, but alfo of art; and that judgment is founded upon obfervation and comparifon.

WHAT

WHAT Horace has faid of Genius, is ftill more applicable to Tafte.

Naturâ fieret laudabile carmen, an arte,
Quæfitum eft. Ego nec ftudium fine divite venâ:
Nec rude quid profit video ingenium: alterius fic
Altera pofcit opem res, & conjurat amicè.

HOR. ART. POET.

'Tis long difputed, whether poets claim
From *Art* or *Nature* their beft right to fame ;
But *Art,* if not enrich'd by Nature's vein,
And a rude *Genius* of uncultur'd ftrain,
Are ufelefs both ; but, when in friendfhip join'd,
A mutual fuccour in each other find.

FRANCIS.

We have feen *Genius* fhine without the help of *Art* ; but *Tafte* muft be cultivated by Art, before it will produce agreeable fruit. This, however, we muft ftill inculcate with Quintilian, that ftudy, precept, and obfervation, will nought avail, without the affiftance of nature :

Illud tamen imprimis teftandum eft, nihil præcepta atque artes valere, nifi adjuvante naturâ.

YET even though Nature has done her part, by implanting the feeds of tafte, great pains muft be taken, and great fkill exerted, in raifing them to a proper pitch of vegetation. The judicious

Tutor

Tutor muſt gradually and tenderly unfold the mental faculties of the Youth committed to his charge.
He muſt cheriſh his delicate perception; ſtore his
mind with proper ideas; point out the different
channels of obſervation; teach him to compare
objects; to eſtabliſh the limits of right and wrong,
of truth and falſehood; to diſtinguiſh beauty from
tinſel, and grace from affectation; in a word,
to ſtrengthen and improve by culture, experience,
and inſtruction, thoſe natural powers of feeling
and ſagacity, which conſtitute the faculty called
TASTE, and enable the profeſſor to enjoy the delights of the BELLES LETTRES.

WE cannot agree in opinion with thoſe who
imagine that Nature has been equally favourable to
all men, in conferring upon them a fundamental
capacity, which may be improved to all the re-
finement of Taſte and Criticiſm. Every day's experience convinces us of the contrary. Of two
Youths educated under the ſame Preceptor, in-
ſtructed with the ſame care, and cultivated with
the ſame aſſiduity, one ſhall not only comprehend,
but even anticipate the leſſons of his Maſter, by
dint of natural diſcernment; while the other toils
in vain to imbibe the leaſt tincture of inſtruction.
Such indeed is the diſtinction between Genius and
Stupidity, which every man has an opportunity of

ſeeing

feeing among his friends and acquaintance. Not
that we ought too haftily to decide upon the natural
capacities of children, before we have maturely
confidered the peculiarity of difpofition, and the
bias by which Genius may be ftrangely warped
from the common path of education. A Youth
incapable of retaining one rule of grammar, or of
acquiring the leaft knowledge of the claffics, may,
neverthelefs, make great progrefs in mathematics ;
nay, he may have a ftrong genius for the mathematics, without being able to comprehend a de-
monftration of Euclid ; becaufe his mind conceives
in a peculiar manner, and is fo intent upon contemplating the objeⅽt in one particular point of
view, that it cannot perceive it in any other. We
have known an inftance of a Boy, who, while his
Mafter complained that he had not capacity to comprehend the properties of a right-angled triangle,
had aⅽtually, in private, by the power of his genius, formed a mathematical fyftem of his own,
difcovered a feries of curious theorems, and even
applied his deduⅽtions to praⅽtical machines of
furprifing conftruⅽtion. Befides, in the education of Youth, we ought to remember, that fome
capacities are like the *pyra præcocia* ; they foon
blow, and foon attain to all that degree of maturity which they are capable of acquiring ; while,
on the other hand, there are geniufes of flow
growth,

growth, that are late in burſting the bud and long
in ripening.   Yet the firſt ſhall yield a faint bloſ-
ſom and inſipid fruit; whereas the produce of the
other ſhall be diſtinguiſhed and admired for its well-
concoćted juice and exquiſite flavour.   We have
known a Boy of five years of age ſurpriſe every
body by playing on the violin in ſuch a manner
as ſeemed to promiſe a prodigy in muſic.   He had
all the aſſiſtance that Art could afford; by the age
of ten, his genius was at the ακμή; yet after that
period, notwithſtanding the moſt intenſe applica-
tion, he never gave the leaſt ſigns of improvement.   At ſix he was admired as a miracle of
muſic; at ſix and twenty, he was neglećted as an
ordinary fidaler.   The celebrated DEAN SWIFT was
a remarkable inſtance in the other extreme.   He
was long conſidered as an incorrigible dunce, and
did not obtain his degree at the Univerſity but
ex ſpeciali gratia: yet when his powers began to
unfold, he ſignalized himſelf by a very remarkable
ſuperiority of genius.   When a Youth, therefore,
appears dull of apprehenſion, and ſeems to derive
no advantage from ſtudy and inſtrućtion, the Tutor muſt exerciſe his ſagacity in diſcovering whether the ſoil be abſolutely barren, or ſown with ſeed
repugnant to its nature, or of ſuch a quality as
requires repeated culture and length of time to
let its juices in fermentation.   Theſe obſervations,
however,

however, relate to Capacity in general, which we
ought carefully to diftinguifh from Tafte. Capacity implies the power of retaining what is received ; Tafte is the power of relifhing or rejecting whatever is offered for the entertainment of
the imagination. A man may have capacity to
acquire what is called Learning and Philofophy ;
but he muft have alfo fenfibility before he feels
thofe emotions with which Tafte receives the im-
preffions of beauty.

NATURAL Tafte is apt to be feduced and debauched by vicious precept and bad example.
There is a dangerous tinfel in falfe Tafte, by which
the unwary mind and young imagination are often fafcinated. Nothing has been fo often explained, and yet fo little underftood, as fimplicity
in writing. Simplicity in this acceptation has a
larger fignification than either the ἁπλόον of the
Greeks, or the *fimplex* of the Latins ; for it implies beauty. It is the ἁπλόον καὶ ἡδύν of Demetrius
Phalereus, the *fimplex munditiis* of Horace, and
expreffed by one word, *naiveté* in the French
language. It is, in fact, no other than beautiful
nature, without affectation or extraneous ornament. In ftatuary, it is the Venus of Medicis ;
in architecture, the Pantheon. It would be an
endlefs tafk to enumerate all the inftances of this

natural

natural fimplicity that occur in poetry and painting, among the antients and moderns. We fhall only mention two examp'es of it, the beauty of which confifts in the pathetic.

ANAXAGORAS, the philofopher and preceptor of Pericles, being told that both his fons were dead, laid his hand upon his heart, and, after a fhort paufe, confoled himfelf with a reflection couched in three words, ἤδειν ϑνητὸς γιγνημκώς, " I knew they were mortal." The other inftance we felect from the tragedy of Macbeth. The gallant Macduff, being informed that his wife and children were murdered by order of the tyrant, pulls his hat over his eyes, and his internal agony burfts out into an exclamation of four words, the moft expreffive, perhaps, that ever were uttered : " He has no children." This is the energetic language of fimple nature, which is now grown into difrepute. By the prefent mode of education we are forcibly warped from the bias of nature, and all fimplicity in manners is rejected. We are taught to difguife and diftort our fentiments, until the faculty of thinking is diverted into an unnatural channel ; and we not only relinquifh and forget, but alfo become incapable of our original difpofitions. We are totally changed into creatures of art and affectation. Our perception is abufed, and even our fenfes are perverted. Our minds

lofe their native force and flavour. The imagination, fweated by artificial fire, produces nought
but vapid bloom. The genius, inftead of grow-
ing like a vigorous tree, extending its branches
on every fide, and bearing delicious fruit, refembles
a ftunted yew, tortured into fome wretched form,
projecting no fhade, difplaying no flower, diffufing no fragrance, yielding no fruit, and affording
nothing but a barren conceit for the amufement
of the idle fpectator.

Thus debauched from Nature, how can we
relifh her genuine productions? As well might
a man diftinguifh objects through a prifm, that
prefents nothing but a variety of colours to the
eye; or a maid pining in the green ficknefs prefer a bifcuit to a cinder. It has been often alledged
that the paffions can never be wholly depofited; and
that by appealing to thefe, a good writer will always be able to force himfelf into the hearts of his
readers : but even the ftrongeft paffions are
weakened, nay fometimes totally extinguifhed,
by mutual oppofition, diffipation, and acquired
infenfibility. How often, at the theatre, is the
tear of fympathy and the burft of laughter repreffed
by a ridiculous fpecies of pride, refufing approbation to the author and actor, and renouncing fociety with the audience ? This feeming infenfibility is not owing to any original defect. Nature
has

has ftretched the ftring, though it has long ceafed
to vibrate. It may have been difplaced and diftracted by the violence of pride ; it may have loft
its tone through long difufe ; or be fo twifted or
overftrained, as to produce the moft jarring dif-
cords.

IF fo little regard is paid to Nature when fhe
knocks fo powerfully at the breaft, fhe muft be
altogether neglected and defpifed in her calmer
mood of ferene tranquillity, when nothing appears
to recommend her but fimplicity, propriety, and
innocence. A perfon muft have delicate feelings
that can tafte the celebrated repartee in Terence :
Homo fum ; nihil humani à me alienum puto : " I
am a man ; therefore think I have an intereft in
every thing that concerns humanity." A clear
blue fky fpangled with ftars will prove an infipid
object to eyes accuftomed to the glare of torches and
tapers, gilding and glitter ; eyes that will turn
with difguft from the green mantle of the fpring,
fo gorgeoufly adorned with buds and foliage,
flowers and bloffoms, to contemplate a gaudy filken
robe, ftriped and interfected with unfriendly tints
that fritter the maffes of light and diftract the
vifion, pinked into the moft fantaftic forms,
flounced, and furbelowed, and fringed with all
the littlenefs of art unknown to elegance.

H 2   THOSE

THOSE ears that are offended by the notes of
the thrufh, the blackbird, and the nightingale, will
be regaled and ravifhed by the fqueaking fiddle
touched by a mufician who has no other genius
than that which lies in his fingers : they will even
be entertained with the rattling of coaches, and
the alarming knock by which the doors of fafhionable people are fo loudly diftinguifhed. The
fenfe of fmelling that delights in the fcent of ex-
crementitious animal juices, fuch as mufk, civet,
and urinous falts, will loath the fragrance of new-
mown hay, the fweet-briar, the honey-fuckle,
and the rofe. The organs that are gratified with
the tafte of fickly veal bled into a palfy, cram-
med fowls, and dropfical brawn, peafe without
fubftance, peaches without tafte, and pine-apples
without flavour, will certainly naufeate the native, genuine, and falutary tafte of Welch beef,
Banftead mutton, and barn-door fowls, whofe
juices are concocted by a natural digeftion, and
whofe flefh is confolidated by free air and exercife.
In fuch a total perverfion of the fenfes, the ideas
muft be mifreprefented ; the powers of the imagination diſordered, and the judgment, of confequence, unfound. The difeafe is attended with
a falfe appetite, which the natural food of the mind
will not fatisfy. It will prefer Ovid to Tibullus,
and the rant of Lee to the tendernefs of Otway.

The

The foul finks into a kind of fleepy ideotifm ; and is diverted by toys and baubles, which can only be pleafing to the moft fuperficial curiofity. It is enlivened by a quick fucceffion of trivial objects, that gliften and dance before the eye ; and, like an infant, is kept awake and infpirited by the found of a rattle. It muft not only be d zzled and aroufed, but alfo cheated, hurried, and per- plexed by the artifice of deception, bufinefs, in- tricacy, and intrigue ; a kind of low juggle, which may be termed the legerdemain of Genius.

In this ftate of depravity the mind cannot enjoy, nor, indeed, diftinguifh the charms of natural and moral beauty and decorum The ingenuous blufh of native innocence, the plain language of an- tient faith and fincerity, the cheerful refignation to the will of Heaven, the mutual affection of the Charities, the voluntary refpect paid to fuperior dignity or ftation, the virtue of beneficence, ex- tended even to the brute creation, nay the very crimfon glow of health, and fwelling lines of beauty, are defpifed, detefted, fcorned, and ridi- culed, as ignorance, rudenefs, rufticity, and fuper- ftition. Thus we fee how moral and natural beauty are connected ; and of what importance it is, even to the formation of Tafte, that the manners fhould be feverely fuperintended. This is a tafk

H 3   which

which ought to take the lead of fcience ; for we
will venture to fay, that Virtue is the foundation
of Tafte ; or rather, that Virtue and Tafte are
built upon the fame foundation of fenfibility, and
cannot be disjoined without offering violence to
both. But Virtue muft be informed, and Tafte
inftructed, otherwife they will both remain imperfect and ineffectual :

Qui didicit patriæ quid debeat, et quid amicis,
Quo fit amore parens, quo frater amandus, et hofpes,
Quod fit Confcripti, quod judicis officium, quæ
Fortes in bellum miffi ducis ; ille profectò
Reddere perfonæ fcit convenientia cuique.

The Critic, who with nice difcernment knows.
What to his country and his friends he owes ;
How various Nature warms the human breaft,
To love the parent, brother, friend, or gueft ;
What the great functions of our judges are,
Of Senators, and General fent to war ;
He can diftinguifh, with unerring art,
The ftrokes peculiar to each different part.

HOR.

Thus we fee Tafte is compofed of Nature improved by Art ; of Feeling tutored by Inftruc-
tion.

ESSAY

E S S A Y   XIV.

HAVING explained what we conceive to be True Taſte, and in ſome meaſure accounted for the prevalence of Vitiated Taſte, we ſhall proceed to point out the moſt effectual manner in which a natural capacity may be improved into a delicacy of judgment, and an intimate acquaintance with the BELLES LETTRES. We ſhall take it for granted that proper means have been uſed to form the manners, and attach the mind to virtue. The heart cultivated by precept, and warmed by example, improves in ſenſibility, which is the foundation of Taſte. By diſtinguiſhing the influence and ſcope of morality, and cheriſhing the ideas of benevolence, it acquires a habit of ſympathy which tenderly feels reſponſive, like the vibration of uniſons, every touch of moral beauty. Hence it is that a man of a ſocial heart, entendered by the practice of virtue, is awakened to the moſt pathetic emotions by every uncommon inſtance of generoſity, compaſſion, and greatneſs of ſoul. Is

there

there any man fo dead to Sentiment, fo loft to
Humanity, as to read unmoved the generous behaviour of the Romans to the States of Greece,
as it is recounted by Livy, or embellifhed by
Thomfon in his Poem of Liberty? Speaking
of Greece in the decline of her power, when her
freedom no longer exifted, he fays :

As at her Ifthmian games, a fading pomp !
Her full-affembled youth innumerous fwarm'd,
On a tribunal rais'd * FLAMINIUS fat ;
A victor he from the deep Phalanx pierc'd
Of iron-coated Macedon, and back
The Grecian tyrant to his bounds repell'd.
In the high thoughtlefs gaiety of game,
While fport alone their unambitious hearts
Poffefs'd ; the fudden trumpet founding hoarfe,
Bad filence o'er the bright affembly reign.
Then thus a herald—" To the ftates of Greece
The Roman People, unconfin'd, reftore
Their countries, cities, liberties, and laws ;
Taxes remit, and garrifons withdraw."
The crowd, aftonifh'd half, and half inform'd,
Star'd dubious round ; fome queftion'd, fome exclaim'd,
(Like one who dreaming, between hope and fear,
Is loft in anxious joy) " Be that again,
—Be that again proclaim'd diftinct and loud !"
Loud and diftinct it was again proclaim'd ;
And ftill as midnight in the rural fhade,
When the gale flumbers, they the words devour'd.
Awhile fevere amazement held them mute,

    * His real name was QUINTUS FLAMINIUS.

Then

Then burfting broad, the boundlefs fhout to heav'n
From many a thoufand hearts extatic fprung!
On ev'ry hand rebellow'd to them joy;
The fwelling fea, the rocks and vocal hills—
—Like Bacchanals they flew,
Each other ftraining in a ftrict embrace,
Nor ftrain'd a flave; and loud acclaims, 'till n'ght,
Round the Proconful's tent repeated rung.

To one acquainted with the Genius of Greece, the character and difpofition of that polifhed peo‐ple, admired for fcience, renowned for an unex‐tinguifhable love of freedom, nothing can be more affecting than this inftance of generous magnani‐mity of the Roman People, in reftoring them, unafked, to the full fruition of thofe liberties which they had fo unfortunately loft.

The mind of Senfibility is equally ftruck by the generous confidence of Alexander, who drinks without hefitation the potion prefented by his phyfician Philip, even after he had received inti‐mation that poifon was contained in the cup : a noble and pathetic fcene! which hath acquired new dignity and expreffion under the inimitable pencil of a Le Sueur.   Humanity is melted into tears of tender admiration by the deportment of Henry IV. of France, while his rebellious fubjects com‐pelled him to form the blockade of his capital. In

H 5   chaftning

chaſtiſing his enemies, he could not but remember they were his people ; and knowing they were
reduced to the extremity of famine, he generouſly
connived at the methods practiſed to ſupply them
with proviſion. Chancing one day to meet two peaſants who had been detected in theſe practices, as
they were led to execution they implored his clemency, declaring in the ſight of Heaven, they had
no other way to procure ſubſiſtence for their wives
and children. He pardoned them on the ſpot, and,
giving them all the money that was in his purſe,
" Henry of Bearne is poor (ſaid he) ; had he more
money to afford, you ſhould have it—go home to
your families in peace ; and remember your duty
to God, and your allegiance to your Sovereign."
Innumerable examples of the ſame kind may be
ſelected from hiſtory, both antient and modern,
the ſtudy of which we would therefore ſtrenuouſly
recommend.

HISTORICAL knowledge, indeed, becomes neceſſary on many other accounts, which in its place
we will explain : but as the formation of the
heart is of the firſt conſequence, and ſhould pre-
cede the cultivation of the underſtanding, ſuch
ſtriking inſtances of ſuperior virtue ought to be
culled for the peruſal of the young pupil, who will
read them with eagerneſs, and revolve them with
pleaſure.

pleafure. Thus the young mind becomes enamoured of moral beauty, and the paffions are
lifted on the fide of humanity. Meanwhile knowledge of a different fpecies will go hand in hand
with the advances of morality, and the underftanding be gradually extended. Virtue and fentiment
reciprocally affift each other, and both conduce to
the improvement of perception. While the fcholar's chief attention is emploved in learning the
Latin and Greek languages, and this is generally
the tafk of childhood and early youth, it is even then
the bufinefs of the Preceptor to give his mind a
turn for obfervation, to direct his powers of difcernment, to point out the diftinguifhing marks of
character, and dwell upon the charms of moral
and intellectual beauty, as they may chance to
occur in the Claffics that are ufed for his inftruc-
tion. In reading Cornelius Nepos and Plutarch's
Lives, even with a view to grammatical improvement only, he will infenfibly imbibe and
learn to compare ideas of greater importance. He
will become enamoured of virtue and patriotifm,
and acquire a deteftation for vice, cruelty, and
corruption. The perufal of the Roman ftory in
the works of Florus, Salluft, Livy, and Taci-
tus, will irrefiftibly eng. ge his attention, expand
his conception, cherifh his memory, exercife his
judgement, and warm him with a noble fpirit of

emula-

emulation. He will contemplate with love and admiration the difintereſted candour of Ariſtides, ſurnamed the Juſt, whom the guilty cabals of his rival Themiſtocles exiled from his ungrateful country by a ſentence of Oſtracifm. He will be ſurprifed to learn, that one of his fellow-citizens, an illiterate artifan, bribed by his enemies, chancing to meet him in the ſtreet without knowing his perfon, defired he would write Ariſtides on his ſhell (which was the method thofe plebeians ufed to vote againſt delinquents),when the innocent patriot wrote his own name without complaint or expoſtulation. He will with equal aſtoniſhment applaud the inflexible integrity of Fabricius, who preferred the poverty of innocence to all the pomp of affluence with which Pyrrhus endeavoured to feduce him from the arms of his country. He will approve with tranſport the noble generofity of his foul in rejecting the propofal of that Prince's phyfician, who offered to take him off by poifon ; and in fending the caitiff bound to his fovereign, whom he would have fo balely and cruelly betrayed.

IN reading the antient authors, even for the purpofes of fchool education, the unformed Taſte will begin to reliſh the irrefiſtible energy, greatnefs and fublimity of Homer, the ferene majeſty, the melody and pathos of Virgil,

the

the tendernefs of Sappho and Tibullus, the elegance and propriety of Terence ; the grace, vivacity, fatire, and fentiment of Horace.

NOTHING will more conduce to the improvement of the fcholar in his knowledge of the languages, as well as in Tafte and morality, than his being obliged to tranflate choice parts and paffages of the moft approved Claffics, both poetry and profe, efpecially the latter ; fuch as the orations of Demofthenes and Ifocrates, the Treatife of Longinus on the Sublime, the Commentaries of Cæfar, the Epiftles of Cicero and the Younger Pliny, and the two celebrated fpeeches in the Catilinarian confpiracy, by Salluft. By this practice he will become more intimate with the beauties of the writing and the idioms of the language from which he tranflates ; at the fame time it will form his ftyle, and, by exercifing his talent of expreffion, make him a more perfect mafter of his mother tongue. Cicero tells us, that in tranflating two orations which the moft celebrated orators of Greece pronounced againft each other, he performed this tafk not as a fervile interpreter but as an orator, preferving the fentiments, forms, and figures of the original, but adapting the expreffion to the tafte and manners of the Romans :—
" *In quibus non verbum pro verbo neceffe habui red-*
dere,

dere, fed genus omnium verborum vimque fervavi ;"
in which I did not think it was neceffary to tranflate literally word for word, but I preferved the
natural and full fcope of the whole." Of the fame
opinion was Horace, who fays in his Art of Poetry,

" *Nec verbo verbum curabis reddere fidus Interpres——*

Nor word for word tranflate with painful care——

Neverthelefs, in taking the liberty here granted, we
are apt to run into the other extreme, and fubftitute equivalent thoughts and phrafes, 'till hardly
any features of the original remain. The metaphors of figures, efpecially in poetry, ought to be
as religioufly preferved as the images of painting,
which we cannot alter or exchange without de-
ftroying, or injuring at leaft, the character and
ftyle of the original.

In this manner the Preceptor will fow the feeds
of that Tafte which will foon germinate, rife,
bloffom, and produce perfect fruit by dint of future care and cultivation. In order to reftrain the
luxuriancy of the young imagination, which is apt
to run riot, to enlarge the ftock of ideas, exercife
the reafon, and ripen the judgement, the pupil muft
be engaged in the feverer ftudy of Science. He
muft learn Geometry, which Plato recommends

for

for ſtrengthening the mind, and enabling it to think with preciſion. He muſt be made acquainted with Geography and Chronology, and trace Philoſophy through all her branches. Without Geography and Chronology he will not be able to acquire a diſtinct idea of Hiſtory ; nor judge of the propriety of many intereſting ſcenes, and a thouſand alluſions that preſent themſelves in the works of Genius. Nothing opens the mind ſo much as the reſearches of Philoſophy ; they inſpire us with ſublime conceptions of the Creator, and ſubject, as it were, all Nature to our command. Theſe beſtow that liberal turn of thinking, and in a great meaſure contribute to that univerſality in learning by which a man of Taſte ought to be eminently diſtinguiſhed. But Hiſtory is the inexhauſtible ſource from which he will derive his moſt uſeful knowledge, reſpecting the progreſs of the human mind, the conſtitution of government, the riſe and decline of empires, the revolution of Arts, the variety of Character, and the viciſſitudes of Fortune.

THE knowledge of Hiſtory enables the Poet not only to paint characters, but alſo to deſcribe magnificent and intereſting ſcenes of battle and adventure. Not that the Poet or Painter ought to be reſtrained to the letter of hiſtorical truth. Hiſtory

repre-

reprefents what has really happened in Nature;
the other Arts exhibit what might have happened,
with fuch exaggeration of circumftance and feature as may be deemed an improvement on Nature : but this exaggeration muft not be carried
beyond the bounds of probability ; and thefe, generally fpeaking, the knowledge of Hiftory will
afcertain. It would be extremely difficult, if not
impoffible, to find a man actually exifting, whofe
proportions fhould anfwer to thofe of the Greek
ftatue diftinguifhed by the name of the Apollo
of Belvedere ; or to produce a woman fimilar in
proportion of parts to the other celebrated piece
called the Venus de Medicis ; therefore it may
be truly affirmed, that they are not conformable to
the real ftandard of Nature : neverthelefs, every
Artift will own that they are the very archetypes
of grace, elegance, and fymmetry ; and every
judging eye muft behold them with admiration
as improvements on the lines and lineaments of
Nature. The truth is, the fculptor or ftatuary compofed the various proportions in Nature from a
great number of different fubjects, every individual of which he found imperfect or defective in
fome one particular, though beautiful in all the
reft ; and from thefe obfervations, corroborated
by tafte and judgement, he formed an ideal pat-
tern according to which his idea was modelled,
and produced in execution.

EVERY

EVERY body knows the ſtory of Zeuxis, the famous painter of Heraclea, who, according to
Pliny, invented the *chiaro oſcuro*, or diſpoſition of
light and ſhade, among the ancients, and excelled
all his cotemporaries in the chromatique, or art
of colouring. This great artiſt being employed
to draw a perfect beauty in the character of He-
len, to be placed in the Temple of Juno, culled
out five of the moſt beautiful damſels the city
could produce, and, ſelecting what was excellent
in each, combined them in one picture according
to the predifpoſition of his fancy, ſo that it ſhone
forth an amazing model of perfection *. In like
manner, every man of Genius, regulated by true
Taſte, entertains in his imagination an ideal
beauty, conceived and cultivated as an improvement upon Nature : and this we refer to the article of Invention.

IT is the buſineſs of Art to imitate Nature, but
not with a ſervile pencil; and to chuſe thoſe atti-

---

* Præbete quæfo, inquit, ex iſtis virginibus formoſiſſimas,
dum pingo id quod pollicitus ſum vobis, ut mutum in ſimu-
lacrum ex animali exemplo veritas transferatur. Ille autem
quinque delegit. Neque enim putavit omnia quæ quærere
ad venuſtatem uno in corpore ſe reperire poſſe ; ideo quod
nihil ſimplici in genere omnibus ex partibus perfectum natura expolivit. CIC. Lib. 2. de Inv. cap. 1.

tudes

tudes and difpofitions only, which are beautiful
and engaging. With this view we muft avoid all
difagreeable profpects of Nature which excite the
ideas of abhorrence and difguft. For example, a
Painter would not find his account in exhibiting
the refemblance of a dead carcafe half confumed by
vermin, or of fwine wallowing in ordure, or of a
beggar loufing himfelf on a dunghill, though
thefe fcenes fhould be painted never fo naturally,
and all the world muft allow that the fcenes were
taken from Nature, becaufe the merit of the
imitation would be greatly over-balanced by the
vile choice of the Artift. There are, neverthelefs, many fcenes of horror which pleafe in
the reprefentation, from a certain interefting
greatnefs which we fhall endeavour to explain,
when we come to confider the Sublime.

WERE we to judge every production by the ri-
gorous rules of Nature, we fhould reject the Iliad
of Homer, the Æneid of Virgil, and every celebrated tragedy of antiquity and the prefent times,
becaufe there is no fuch thing in Nature as an
Hector or Turnus talking in hexameter, or an
Othello in blank verfe : we fhould condemn the
Hercules of Sophocles, and the Mifer of Moliere,
becaufe we never knew a hero fo ftrong as the one,
or a wretch fo fordid as the other. But if we confider

fider Poetry as an elevation of natural dialogue, as a delightful vehicle for conveying the nobleft fentiments of heroifm and patriot virtue, to re-gale the fenfe with the founds of mufical expref-fion, while the fancy is ravifhed with enchanting images, and the heart warmed to rapture and ex-tafy, we muft allow that Poetry is a perfection to which Nature would gladly afpire ; and that though it furpaffes, it does not deviate from her, provided the characters are marked with propriety and fuftained with Genius. Characters there-fore, both in Poetry and Painting, may be a little overcharged or exaggerated without offering vio-lence to Nature ; nay, they muft be exaggerated in order to be ftriking, and to preferve the idea of Imitation, from whence the reader and fpectator derive in many inftances their chief delight. If we meet a common acquaintance in the ftreet, we fee him without emotion ; but fhould we chance to fpy his portrait well executed, we are ftruck with pleafing admiration. In this cafe the plea-fure arifes entirely from the Imitation. We every day hear unmoved the natives of Ireland and Scot-land fpeaking their own dialects ; but fhould an Englifhman mimic either, we are apt to burft out into a loud laugh of applaufe, being furprifed and tickled by the Imitation alone; though, at the fame time, we cannot but allow that the Imitation

is

is imperfect. We are more affected by reading
Shakefpeare's defcription of Dover Cliff, and Otway's Picture of the Old Hag, than we fhould be,
were we actually placed on the fummit of the one,
or met in reality with fuch a beldame as the other;
becaufe in reading thefe defcriptions we refer to
our own experience, and perceive with furprife the
juftnefs of the Imitations. But if it is fo clofe as
to be miftaken for Nature, the pleafure then will
ceafe, becaufe the μίμησις; or Imitation no longer
appears.

ARISTOTLE fays, that all Poetry and Mufic is
Imitation *, whether epic, tragic, or comic,
whether vocal or inftrumental, from the pipe or
the lyre. He obferves, that in man there is a
propenfity to imitate even from his infancy; that
the firft perceptions of the mind are acquired by
Imitation; and feems to think that the pleafure derived from Imitation is the gratification of an appetite implanted by Nature. We fhould rather
think the pleafure it gives, arifes from the mind's
contemplating that excellency of Art which thus

---

* Εποποιία δη και η της τραγωδίας ποίησις, έτι δε κωμωδία
και η διθυραμβοποιητικη, και της αυλιτικη; η πλείςη και
κιθαρισικης, πάσαι τογχανουσιν ουσαι μιμη; εις το σινολον.

rivals

rivals Nature, and feems to vie with her in creat-
ing fuch a ftriking refemblance of her works.
Thus the Arts may be juftly termed Imitative,
even in the article of Invention : for, in forming
a character, contriving an incident, and defcribing a fcene, he muft ftill keep Nature in view, and
refer every particular of his invention to her
ftandard ; otherwife his production will be deftitute of truth and probability, without which the
beauties of Imitation cannot fubfift.　It will be a
monfter of incongruity, fuch as Horace alludes
to, in the beginning of his Epiftle to the Pifos :

Humano capiti cervicem pictor equinam
Jungere fi velit, & varias inducere plumas
Undique collatis membris, ut turpiter atrum
Definat in pifcem, mulier formofa fuperne !
Spectatum admiffi ; rifum teneatis, amici ?

Suppofe a painter to a human head
Should join a horfe's neck, and wildly fpread
The various plumage of the feather'd kind
O'er limbs of different beafts abfurdly join'd ;
Or if he gave to view a beauteous maid
Above the waift with every charm array'd ;
Should a foul fifh her lower parts unfold,
Would you not laugh fuch pictures to behold ?

THE magazine of Nature fupplies all thofe
images which compofe the moft beautiful Imitations.

tions. This the Artift examines occafionally, as he would confult a collection of mafterly fketches; and, felecting particulars for his purpofe, mingles the ideas with a kind of enthufiafm, or τὶ Θεῖον, which is that gift of heaven we call Genius, and finally produces fuch a whole, as commands admiration and applaufe.

ESSAY

E S S A Y   XV.

THE ſtudy of Polite Literature is generally ſuppoſed to include all the Liberal Arts of Poetry, Painting, Sculpture, Muſic, Eloquence, and
Architecture. All theſe are founded on imitation :
and all of them mutually aſſiſt and illuſtrate each
other. But as Painting, Sculpture, Muſic, and
Architecture, cannot be perfectly attained without
long practice of manual operation, we ſhall dif-
tinguiſh them from Poetry and Eloquence, which
depend entirely on the faculties of the mind ; and
on theſe laſt, as on the Arts, which immediately
conſtitute the BELLES LETTRES, employ our attention in the preſent enquiry : or, if it ſhould
run to a greater length than we propoſe, it ſhall be
confined to Poetry alone; a ſubject that comprehends in its full extent the province of Taſte, or
what is called Polite Literature; and differs eſſen-
tially from Eloquence, both in its end and origin.

POETRY ſprung from eaſe, and was conſecrated
to pleaſure ; whereas Eloquence aroſe from neceſ-
ſity, and aims at conviction. When we ſay Poetry

try fprang from eafe, perhaps we ought to except
that fpecies of it which owed its rife to infpira-
tion and enthufiafin, and properly belonged to the
culture of religion. In the firft ages of mankind,
and even in the original ftate of Nature, the un-
lettered mind muft have been ftruck with fublime
conceptions, with admiration and awe, by thofe
great phænomena, which, though every day repeated, can never be viewed without internal emotion. Thofe would break forth in exclamations
expreffive of the paffion produced, whether furprife or gratitude, terror or exultation. The
rifing, the apparent courfe, the fetting, and feeming renovation of the fun ; the revolution of light
and darknefs ; the fplendour, change,ʼ and circuit of the moon, and the canopy of heaven be-
fpangled with ftars, muft have produced expreffions of wonder and adoration. " O glorious lu-
minary ! great eye of the world ! fource of that
light which guides my fteps ! of that heat which
warms me when chilled with cold! of that influence
which chears the face of Nature ! whither doft
thou retire every evening with the fhades ?
Whence doft thou fpring every morning with re-
novated luftre, and never-fading glory ? Art not
thou the ruler, the creator, the God, of all that
I behold ? I adore thee, as thy child, thy flave, thy
fuppliant ! I crave thy protection, and the conti- ·

nuance of thy goodnefs ! Leave me not to perifh with cold, or to wander folitary in utter
darknefs ! Return, return, after thy wonted abfence : drive before thee the gloomy clouds that
would obfcure the face of Nature. The birds begin to warble, and every animal is filled with glad-
nefs at thy approach : even the trees, the herbs,
and the flowers, feem to rejoice with frefher beauties, and fend forth a grateful incenfe to thy
power, from whence their origin is derived !"
A number of individuals, infpired with the fame
ideas, would join in thefe orifons, which would
be accompanied with correfponding gefticulations
of the body. They would be improved by practice, and grow regular from repetition. The
founds and geftures would naturally fall into
meafured cadence. Thus the fong and dance
would be produced ; and a fyftem of worfhip being formed, the Mufe would be confecrated to
the purpofes of religion.

HENCE thofe forms of thankfgivings, and lita-
nies of fupplication, with which the religious
rites of all nations, even the moft barbarous, are
at this day celebrated in every quarter of the
known world. Indeed this is a circumftance in
which all nations furprifingly agree, how much
foever they may differ in every other article of

laws, cuftoms, manners, and religion. The antient Egyptians celebrated the feftivals of their
god Apis with hymns and dances. The fuperftition of the Greeks, partly derived from the
Egyptians, abounded with poetical ceremonies,
fuch as chorus's and hymns, fung and danced at
their apotheofes, facrifices, games, and divina-
tions. The Romans had their *carmen feculare,* and
Salian priefts, who, on certain feftivals, fung
and danced through the ftreets of Rome. The
Ifraelites were famous for this kind of exultation:
" And Miriam the prophetefs, the fifter of
Aaron, took a timbrel in her hand, and all the
women went out after her, with timbrels and
with dances, and Miriam anfwered them, Sing
ye to the Lord, &c."—" And David danced before the Lord with all his might."—The pfalms
compofed by this monarch, the fongs of Deborah
and Ifaiah, are farther confirmations of what we
have advanced.

From the Phœnicians the Greeks borrowed
the curted Orthyan fong, when they facrificed
their children to Diana. The Poetry of the
Bards conftituted great part of the religious ceremonies among the Gauls and Britons; and the
caroufals of the Goths were religious inftitutions,
celebrated with fongs of triumph. The Mahome-

tan Dervife dances to the found of the flute,
and whirls himfelf round until he grows giddy,
and falls into a trance. Their Marabous compofe
hymns in praife of Allah. The Chinefe celebrate
their grand feftivals with proceffions of idols,
fongs, and inftrumental mufic. The Tartars,
Samoiedes, Laplanders, Negroes, even the Caf-
fres called Hottentots, folemnize their worfhip
(fuch as it is) with fongs and dancing ; fo that we
may venture to fay, Poetry is the univerfal vehicle in which all nations have expreffed their moft
fublime conceptions.

POETRY was, in all appearance, previous to
any concerted plan of worfhip, and to every
eftablifhed fyftem of legiflation. When certain
individuals, by dint of fuperior prowefs or underftanding, had acquired the veneration of their fellow favages, and erected themfelves into divinities
on the ignorance and fuperftition of mankind;
then mythology took place, and fuch a fwarm of
deities arofe, as produced a religion replete with
the moft fhocking abfurdities. Thofe whom their
fuperior talents had deified, were found to be ftill
actuated by the moft brutal paffions of human nature ; and, in all probability, their votaries were
glad to find fuch examples to countenance their
own vicious inclinations. Thus fornication, in-

I 2   ceft,

ceft, rape, and even beftiality, were fanctified by
the amours of Jupiter, Pan, Mars, Venus, and
Apollo. Theft was patronized by Mercury;
drunkennefs by Bacchus; and cruelty by Diana.
The fame heroes and legiflators, thofe who delivered their country, founded cities, eftablifhed
focieties, invented ufeful arts, or contributed in
any eminent degree to the fecurity and happinefs
of their fellow-creatures, were infpired by the
fame lufts and appetites which domineered among
the inferior claffes of mankind; therefore every
vice incident to human nature was celebrated in
the worfhip of one or other of thefe divinities; and
every infirmity consecrated by public feaft and folemn facrifice. In thefe inftitutions the Poet
bore a principal fhare. It was his genius that
contrived the plan, that executed the form of
worfhip, and recorded in verfe the origin and
adventures of their gods and demi-gods. Hence
the impurities and horrors of certain rites; the
groves of Paphos and Baal-Peor; the orgies of
Bacchus; the human facrifices to Moloch and
Diana. Hence the theogony of Hefiod; the
theology of Homer; and thofe innumerable
maxims fcattered through the antient Poets, in-
viting mankind to gratify their fenfual appetites,
in imitation of the gods, who were certainly the
beft judges of happinefs. It is well known, that

Plato

Plato expelled Homer from his commonwealth, on account of the infamous characters by which he hath diftinguifhed his deities; as well as for fome depraved fentiments which he found diffufed through the courfe of the Iliad and Odyffey. Cicero enters into the fpirit of Plato, and exclaims in his firft book *De Natura Deorum, Nec multa abfurdiora funt ea, quæ, poetarum vocibus fufa, ipfa fuavitate nocuerunt : qui, & ira inflammatos, & libidine furentes, induxerunt Deos, feceruntque ut eorum bella, pugnas, prælia, vulnera videremus : vaia præterea, anguis, dijceradas, ortus, interitus, querelas, lamentationes, effufas in omni intemperantiâ libidines, adulteria, vincula, cum humano genere concubitus, mortalefque ex immortali procreatos.* " Nor are thofe things much more abfurd which, flowing from the Poet's tongue, have done mifchief even by the fweetnefs of his expreffion. The Poets have introduced gods inflamed with anger and enraged with luft ; and even produced before our eyes their wars, their wrangling, their duels, and their wounds. They have expofed befides, their antipathies, animofities, and diffenfions ; their origin and death ; their complaints and lamentations ; their appetites, indulged to all manner of excefs, their adul-

teries

teries, their fetters, their amorous commerce with the human species; and from immortal parents derived a mortal offspring."

As the festivals of the gods necessarily produced good cheer, which was often carried to riot and debauchery, mirth of consequence prevailed ; and this was always attended with buffoonery. Taunts and jokes, and raillery and repartee, would necessarily ensue ; and individuals would contend for the victory in wit and genius. These contests would in time be reduced to some regulations, for the entertainment of the people thus assembled, and some prize would be decreed to him who was judged to excel his rivals. The candidates for fame and profit being thus stimulated, would task their talents, and naturally recommend these alternate recriminations to the audience, by clothing them with a kind of poetical measure, which should bear a near resemblance to prose. Thus, as the solemn service of the day was composed in the most sublime species of Poetry, such as the ode or hymn, the subsequent altercation was carried on in Iambics, and gave rise to Satire. We are told by the Stagyrite, that the highest species of Poetry was employed in celebrating great actions ; but the humbler sort used in this kind of

con-

contention * ; and that in the ages of antiquity there were fome bards that profeſſed Heroics, and fome that pretended to Iambics only. Οι μιν ηραἰκῶν, οἱ δὲ ἰάμβων ποιηται.

To theſe rude beginnings we not only owe the birth of Satire, but likewiſe the origin of Dramatic Poetry. Tragedy herſelf, which afterwards attained to ſuch dignity as to rival the Epic Muſe, was at firſt no other than a trial of Crambo, or Iambics, between two peaſants, and a goat was the prize, as Horace calls it, *vile certamen ob hircum;* " a mean conteſt for a he-goat." Hence the name τραγωδία, ſignifying the goat-ſong, from τραγος *hircus,* and ὠδη *carmen.*

Carmine qui tragico vilem certavit ob hircum,
Mox etiam agreſtes ſatyros nudavit, & aſper
Incolumi gravitate jocum tentavit, eo quod
Illecebris erat & gratâ novitate morandus
Spectator, functuſque ſacris, & potus & exlex. Hor.

The tragic bard, a goat his humble prize,
Bade ſatyrs naked and uncouth ariſe ;
His muſe ſevere, ſecure and undiſmay'd,
The ruſtic joke in ſolemn ſtrain convey'd ;
For novelty alone he knew could charm
A lawleſs croud, with wine and feaſting warm.

* Οἱ μιν γαρ σιμνότιροι, τας καλας ιμιμουιτο πραξὶς ——οἱ δὲ ιυτιλισιροι, τας των φαυλων, πρῶτον ψόγοις ἑαυντις.

SATIRE then was originally a clownifh dialogue in loofe Iambics, fo called becaufe the actors were difguifed like fatyrs, who not only recited the praifes of Bacchus, or fome other deity,
but interfperfed their hymns with farcaftic jokes
and altercation.   Of this kind is the *Cyclop* of
Euripides, in which Ulyffes is the principal actor.
The Romans alfo had their *Atellana* or interludes
of the fame nature, fo called from the city of
Atella, where they were firft acted : but thefe
were highly polifhed in comparifon of the original
entertainment, which was altogether rude and
indecent.   Indeed the *Cyclop* itfelf, though compofed by the accomplifhed Euripides, abounds
with fuch impurity, as ought not to appear on the
ftage of any civilized nation.

IT is very remarkable, that the *Atellana*, which
were in effect tragi-comedies, grew into fuch
efteem among the Romans, that the performers
in thefe pieces enjoyed feveral privileges which
were refufed to the ordinary actors.   They were
not obliged to unmafk, like the other players, when
their action was difagreeable to the audience.
They were admitted into the army, and enjoyed
the privileges of free citizens, without incurring
that difgrace which was affixed to the characters

of

of other actors *. The Poet Laberius, who was of equeſtrian order, being preſſed by Julius Cæſar to act a part in his own performance, complied with great reluctance, and complained of the diſhonour he had incurred, in his prologue pre-ſerved by Macrobius, which is one of the moſt elegant morſels of antiquity.

Tragedy and Comedy flowed from the ſame fountain; though their ſtreams were ſoon divided. The ſame entertainment which, under the name of *Tragedy*, was rudely exhibited by clowns, for the prize of a goat, near ſome rural altar of Bacchus, aſſumed the appellation of *Comedy* when it was transferred into cities, and repreſented with a little more decorum in a cart or waggon, that ſtrolled from ſtreet to ſtreet, as the name κωμῳδια implies, being derived from κωμη a ſtreet, and ᾠδη a poem. To this origin Horace alludes in theſe lines :

Dicitur, & plauſtris vexiſſe poemata Theſpis,
Qua canerent agerentque, peruncti fæcibus ora.

Theſpis, inventor of Dramatic art,
Convey'd his vagrant actors in a cart :

* Cum artem ludicram, ſcenamque totam probro duce-rent, genus id hominum non modo honore civium reliquo-rum carere, ſed etiam tribu moveri notatione cenſoria vo-luerunt. *Cic. apud S. Aug. de Civit. Dei.*

High

High o'er the crowd the mimic tribe appear'd,
And play'd and fung, with lees of wine befmear'd.

THESPIS is called the inventor of the Dramatic Art, becaufe he raifed the fubject from
clownifh altercation to the character and exploits
of fome hero : he improved the language and
verfification, and relieved the Chorus by the
dialogue of two actors. This was the firft ad-
vance towards that confummation of Genius and
Art which conftitutes what is now called a perfect Tragedy. The next great improver was
Æfchylus, of whom the fame critic fays,

Poft hunc perfonæ pallæque repertor honeftæ
Æfchylus & modicis inftravit pulpita tignis;
Et docuit magnumque loqui, nitique cothurno.

Then Æfchylus a decent vizard us'd ;
Built a low ftage ; the flowing robe diffus'd :
In language more fublime two actors rage,
And in the graceful bufkin tread the ftage.

THE dialogue which Thefpis introduced was
called the *Epifode,* becaufe it was an addition to
the former fubject, namely, the praifes of Bacchus ;
fo that now Tragedy confifted of two diftinct
parts, independent of each other ; the old *Recita-*
tive, which was the *Chorus,* fung in honour of the
gods ; and the *Epifode,* which turned upon
the

the adventures of fome hero. This Epifode being found very agreeable to the people, Æfchylus, who lived about half a century after Thefpis, ftill improved the drama, united the chorus to the epifode fo as to make them both parts or members of one fable, multiplied the actors, contrived the ftage, and introduced the decorations of the theatre ; fo that Sophocles, who fucceeded Æfchylus, had but one ftep to furmount in order to bring the drama to perfection. Thus Tragedy was gradually detached from its original inftitution, which was entirely religious. The priefts of Bacchus loudly complained of this innovation by means of the Epifode, which was foreign to the intention of the Chorus; and hence arofe the proverb of *Nihil ad Dionyfium,* " nothing to the purpofe." Plutarch himfelf mentions the Epifode as a perverfion of tragedy, from the honour of the Gods to the paffions of men: but, notwithftanding all oppofition, the new Tragedy fucceeded to admiration ; becaufe it was found the moft pleafing vehicle of conveying moral truths, of meliorating the heart, and extending the interefts of humanity.

COMEDY, according to Ariftotle, is the younger fifter of Tragedy. As the firft originally turned upon the praifes of the gods, the latter

I 6   dwelt

dwelt on the follies and vices of mankind. Such, we mean, was the fcope of that fpecies of Poetry which acquired the name of Comedy, in contra-diftinction to the Tragic Mufe; for in the begin-ning they were the fame. The foundation upon whcih Comedy was built we have alread yexplained tobe the practice of fatirical repartee or altercation, in which individuals expofed the follies and frail-ties of each other on public occafions of wor-fhip and feftivity.

THE firft regular plan of Comedy is faid to have been the *Margites* of Homer, expofing the idlenefs and folly of a worthlefs character; but of this performance we have no remains. That divifion which is termed the *Antient Comedy*, belongs to the labours of Eupolis, Cratinus, and Ariftophanes, who were cotemporaries, and flourifhed at Athens about four hundred and thirty years before the Chriftian æra. Such was the licence of the Mufe at this period, that, far from lafhing vice in general characters, fhe boldly ex-hibited the exact portrait of every individual who had rendered himfelf remarkable or notorious by his crimes, folly, and debauchery. She affumed every circumftance of his external appearance, his very attire, air, manner, and even his name; according to the obfervation of Horace,

—————————*Petta*

——————————————————Poetæ
——————quorum Comœdia prifca virorum eſt :
Si quis erat dignus deſcribi, quod malus, aut fur,
Quod mæchus foret, aut ſicarius, aut alioqui
Famoſus, multa cum libertate notabant.

The Comic Poets, in its earlieſt age,
Who form'd the manners of the Grecian ſtage—
Was there a villain who'might juſtly claim
A better right of being damn'd to fame,
Rake, cut-throat, thief, whatever was his crime,
They boldly ſtigmatis'd the wretch in rhime.

Eupolis is ſaid to have ſatirized Alcibíades in this manner, and to have fallen a ſacrifice to the re-ſentment of that powerful Athenian : but others ſay he was drowned in the Hellefpont, during a war againſt the Lacedemonians ; and that, in con-ſequence of this accident, the Athenians paſſed a decree, that no Poet ſhould ever bear arms.

The Comedies of Cratinus are recommended by Quintilian for their eloquence ; and Plutarch tells us, that even Pericles himfelf could not efcape the cenſure of this Poet.

Aristophanes, of whom there are eleven Comedies ſtill extant, enjoyed ſuch a pre-emi-nence of reputation, that the Athenians, by a public decree, honoured him with a crown
made

made of a confecrated olive-tree, which grew in
the citadel, for his care and fuccefs in detecting
and expofing the vices of thofe who governed the
commonwealth. Yet this Poet, whether impel-
led by mere wantonnefs of genius, or actuated
by malice and envy, could not refrain from employing the fhafts of his ridicule againft Socrates,
the moft venerable character of Pagan antiquity.
In the Comedy of The Clouds, this virtuous Philofopher was exhibited on the ftage under his own
name, in a cloak exactly refembling that which
Socrates wore, in a mafk modelled from his features, difputing publickly on the nature of right
and wrong. This was undoubtedly an inftance
of the moft flagrant licentioufnefs ; and what renders it the more extraordinary, the audience received it with great applaufe, even while Socrates
himfelf fat publickly in the theatre. The truth is,
the Athenians were fo fond of ridicule, that they
relifhed it even when employed againft the gods
themfelves, fome of whofe characters were very
roughly handled by Ariftophanes and his rivals
in reputation.

WE might here draw a parallel between the inhabitants of Athens and the natives of England,
in point of conftitution, genius, and difpofition.
Athens was a free ftate like England, that piqued
itfelf

tfelf upon the influence of the democracy. Like England, its wealth and strength depended upon its maritime power; and it generally acted as umpire in the disputes that arose among its neighbours. The people of Athens, like those of England, were remarkably ingenious, and made great progress in the Arts and Sciences. They excelled in Poetry, History, Philosophy, Mechanics, and Manufactures; they were acute, discerning, disputatious, fickle, wavering, rash, and combustible, and, above all other nations in Europe, addicted to ridicule; a character which the English inherit in a very remarkable degree.

If we may judge from the writings of Aristophanes, his chief aim was to gratify the spleen and excite the mirth of his audience; of an audience too that would seem to have been uninformed by Taste, and altogether ignorant of decorum; for his pieces are replete with the most extravagant absurdities, virulent slander, impiety, impurities, and low buffoonery. The Comic Muse, not contented with being allowed to make free with the gods and philosophers, applied her scourge so severely to the magistrates of the commonwealth, that it was thought proper to restrain her within bounds by a law, enacting, that no person should

be

be ftigmatifed under his real name ; and thus the
Chorus was filenced.   In order to elude the pe-
nalty of this law, and gratify the Tafte of the
people, the Poets began to fubftitute fictitious
names,   under which they exhibited particular
characters in fuch lively colours, that the refemblance could not poffibly be miftaken or over-
looked.   This practice gave rife to what is called
the *Middle Comedy*, which was but of fhort duration : for the legiflature, perceiving that the firft
law had not removed the grievance againft which
it was provided, iffued a fecond ordinance, for-
bidding, under fevere penalties, any real or family-
occurrences to be reprefented.   This reftriction
was the immediate caufe of improving Comedy
into a general mirror, held forth to reflect the various follies and foibles incident to Human Nature ; a fpecies of writing called the *New Comedy*,
introduced by Diphilus and Menander, of whofe
works nothing but a few fragments remain.

E S S A Y XVI.

HAVING communicated our fentiments touching the origin of Poetry, by tracing Tragedy and Comedy to their common fource, we fhall now endeavour to point out the criteria, by which Poetry is diftinguifhed from every other fpecies of writing. In common with other Arts, fuch as ftatuary and painting, it comprehends imitation, invention, compofition, and enthufiafm. Imitation is, indeed, the bafis of all the liberal Arts: Invention and Enthufiafm conftitute Genius, in whatever manner it may be difplayed. Eloquence of all forts admits of Enthufiafm. Tully fays, an orator fhould be *vehemens ut procella, excitatus ut torrens, incenfus ut fulmen; tonat, fulgurat, et rapidis eloquentiæ fluctibus cuncta proruit et proturbat.* " Violent as a tempeft, impetuous as a torrent, and glowing intenfe like the red bolt of heaven, he thunders, lightens, overthrows, and bears down all before him, by

the

the irrefiftible tide of Eloquence." This is the
mens divinior atque os. magna fonaturum of Horace. This is the talent,

> ――*Meum qui pectus inaniter angit,*
> *Irritat, mulcet, falfis terroribus implet,*
> *Ut magus.*

> With paffions not my own who fires my heart ;
> Who with unreal terrors fills my breaft,
> As with a magic influence poffeft.

We are told, that Michael Angelo Buonaroti
ufed to work at his ftatues in a fit of enthufiafm,
during which he made the fragments of the ftone
fly about him with furprifing violence. The celebrated Lully being one day blamed for fetting
nothing to mufic but the languid verfes of Qui-
nault, was animated with the reproach, and running in a fit of enthufiafm to his harpfichord, fung
in recitative and accompanied four pathetic lines
from the Iphigenia of Racine with fuch expreffion,
as filled the hearers with aftonifhment and horror.

THOUGH Verfification be one of the criteria
that diftinguifh Poetry from Profe, yet it is not the
fole mark of diftinction. Were the Hiftories of
Polybius and Livy fimply turned into Verfe, they
would not become Poems; becaufe they would
be

be deſtitute of thoſe figures, embelliſhments, and
flights of imagination, which diſplay the Poet's
Art and Invention. On the other hand, we have
many productions that juſtly lay claim to the title
of Poetry, without having the advantage of Verſification ; witneſs the Pſalms of David, the Song
of Solomon, with many beautiful hymns, deſcrip-
tions, and rhapſodies, to be found in different
parts of the Old Teſtament ; ſome of them the
immediate production of divine inſpiration : witneſs the Celtic fragments which have lately appeared in the Engliſh language, and are certainly
replete with poetical merit. But though good
verſification alone will not conſtitute Poetry, bad
verſification alone will certainly degrade and render diſguſtful the ſublimeſt ſentiments and fineſt
flowers of imagination. This humiliating power of
bad Verſe appears in many tranſlations of the antient Poets ; in Ogilby's Homer, Trapp's Virgil,
and frequently in Creech's Horace. This laſt, indeed, is not wholly devoid of ſpirit, but it ſeldom
riſes above mediocrity ; and as Horace ſays,

——*Mediocribus eſſe poetis*
Non homines, non Di, non conceſſere columnæ.

But God and man and letter'd poſt denies.
That Poets ever are of middling ſize.

How

How is that beautiful Ode beginning with " *Juſ-tum & tenacem propoſiti virum,*" chilled and tamed by the following tranſlation :

> He who by principle is ſway'd,
> In truth and juſtice ſtill the ſame,
> Is neither of the crowd afraid,
> Tho' civil broils the ſtate inflame ;
> Nor to a haughty tyrant's frown will ſtoop,
> Nor to a raging ſtorm, when all the winds are up.
>
> Should Nature with convulſions ſhake,
> Struck with the fiery bolts of Jove,
> The final doom and dreadful crack
> Cannot his conſtant courage move.

That long Alexandrine—" Nor to a raging ſtorm, when all the winds are up," is drawling, feeble, ſwoln with a pleonaſm or tautology, as well as deficient in the rhyme ; and as for " the dreadful crack" in the next ſtanza, inſtead of exciting terror, it conveys a low and ludicrous idea. How much more elegant and energetic is this paraphraſe of the ſame Ode, inſerted in one of the volumes of Hume's Hiſtory of England ?

> The man whoſe mind, on virtue bent,
> Purſues ſome greatly good intent
>   With undiverted aim,
> Serene beholds the angry crowd;
> Nor can their clamours fierce and loud
>   His ſtubborn honour tame.

Nor

Nor the proud tyrant's fierceſt threat,
Nor ſtorms that from their dark retreat
　The lawleſs ſurges wake;
Nor Jove's dread bolt that ſhakes the pole,
The firmer purpoſe of his ſoul
　With all its power can ſhake.

Should Nature's frame in ruins fall,
And Chaos o'er the ſinking ball
　Reſume primæval ſway,
His courage chance and fate defies,
Nor feels the wreck of earth and ſkies
　Obſtruct its deſtin'd way.

IF Poetry exiſts independent of verſification, it will naturally be aſked, how then is it to be diſtinguiſhed? Undoubtedly, by its own peculiar expreſſion: it has a language of its own, which ſpeaks ſo feelingly to the heart, and ſo pleaſingly to the imagination, that its meaning cannot poſſibly be miſunderſtood by any perſon of delicate ſenſations. It is a ſpecies of painting with words, in which the figures are happily conceived, ingeniouſly arranged, affectingly expreſſed, and recommended with all the warmth and harmony of colouring: it conſiſts of imagery, deſcription, metaphors, ſimiles, and ſentiments, adapted with propriety to the ſubject, ſo contrived and executed as to ſooth the ear, ſurpriſe and delight the fancy,

mend

'mend and melt the heart, elevate the mind, and
pleaſe the underſtanding. According to Flaccus,

> *Aut prodeſſe voluxt, aut deleſtare poëtæ ;*
> *Aut ſimul & jucunda & idonea dicere vitæ.*

Poets would profit or delight mankind,
And with th'amuſing ſhew the inſtructive join'd—

> *Omne tulit punſtum, qui miſcuit utile dulci,*
> *Leſtorem deleſtando, pariterque monendo.*

Profit and pleaſure mingled thus with Art,
To footh the fancy and improve the heart.—

TROPES and figures are likewiſe liberally uſed
in Rhetoric ; and ſome of the moſt celebrated
orators have owned themſelves much indebted to
the Poets. Theophraſtus expreſsly recommends
the Poets for this purpoſe. From their ſource
the ſpirit and energy, the pathetic, the ſublime,
and the beautiful, are derived *. But theſe figures
muſt be more ſparingly uſed in Rhetoric than in
Poetry, and even then mingled with argumentation, and a detail of facts altogether different from
Poetical narration. The Poet, inſtead of ſimply

---

* Namque ab his (ſcilicet poetis) et in rebus ſpiritus, et
in verbis ublimitas, et in affectibus motus omnis, et in per-
ſonis decor petitur.   QUINTILIAN, l. x.

relating

relating the incident, ftrikes off a glowing picture of the fcene, and exhibits it in the moft
lively colours to the eye of the imagination. " It
is reported that Homer was blind (fays Tully in
his Tufculan Queftions), yet his Poetry is no other
than Painting. What country, what climate,
what ideas, battles, commotions, and contefts of
men, as well as of wild beafts, has he not painted
in fuch a manner as to bring before our eyes
thofe very fcenes which he himfelf could not be-
'hold * ?" We cannot, therefore, fubfcribe to the
opinion of fome ingenious critics, who have
blamed Mr. Pope for deviating in fome inftances
'from the fimplicity of Homer, in his tranflation
of the Iliad and Odyffey. For example, the Grecian bard fays fimply, the fun rofe; and his Tranflator gives us a beautiful picture of the fun rifing.
Homer mentions a perfon who played upon the .
lyre ; the Tranflator fets him before us warbling
to the filver ftrings. If this be a deviation, it is
at the fame time an improvement. Homer himfelf, as Cicero obferves above, is full of this kind
of painting, and particularly fond of defcription,
even in fituations where the action feems to re-
quire hafte. Neptune, obferving from Samothrace

* Quæ regio, quæ ora, quæ fpecies formæ, quæ pugna,
qui malus hominum, qui ferarum, non ita expictus eft, ut
quæ ipfe non viderit, nos ut videremus, effeccrit ?

the

the difcomfiture of the Grecians before Troy, flies to their affiftance, and might have been wafted thither in half a line : but the bard de-fcribes him, firft, defcending the mountain on which he fat ; fecondly, ftriding towards his pa-lace at Ægæ, and yoking his horfes ; thirdly, he defcribes him putting on his armour ; and laftly, afcending his car, and driving along the furface of the fea. Far from being difgufted by thefe de-lays, we are delighted with the particulars of the defcription. Nothing can be more fublime than the circumftance of the mountain's trembling be-neath the footfteps of an immortal,

$$\text{—— } T\varrho\acute{\iota}\mu\iota \; \delta' \; \ddot{\upsilon}\varrho\iota\alpha \; \mu\alpha\varkappa\varrho\grave{\alpha} \; \varkappa\alpha\iota \; \ddot{\upsilon}\lambda\eta$$
$$\Pi o\sigma\sigma\grave{\iota}\nu \; \dot{\upsilon}\pi' \; \dot{\alpha}\vartheta\alpha\nu\acute{\alpha}\tau o\iota\sigma\iota \; \Pi o\sigma\iota\delta\acute{\alpha}\omega\nu\Theta \cdot \; \ddot{\iota}o\nu\tau\Theta.$$

But his paffage to the Grecian fleet is altogether tranfporting.

$$B\tilde{\eta}\delta' \; \dot{\iota}\lambda\acute{\alpha}\omega\nu \; \dot{\epsilon}\pi\iota \; \varkappa\acute{\upsilon}\mu\alpha\tau' \; \&c.$$

He mounts the car, the golden fcourge applies,
He fits fuperior, and the chariot flies ;
His whirling wheels the glaffy furface fweep :
Th' enormous monfters, rolling o'er the deep,
Gambol around him on the watery way,
And heavy whales in aukward meafures play :
The fea fubfiding fpreads a level plai ı,
Exults and crowns the monarch of the main :
The parting waves before his courfers fly :
The wond'ring waters leave his axle dry.—

WITH

WITH great veneration for the memory of Mr. Pope, we cannot help objecting to some lines of this translation We have no idea of the sea's exulting and crowning Neptune, after it had subsided into a level plain.   There is no such image in the original.   Homer says, the whales exulted, and knew or owned their king; and that the sea parted with joy: γηθοσύνη δὲ θάλασσα διίστατο. Neither is there a word of the wondering waters: we, therefore, think the lines might be thus altered to advantage.

> They knew and own'd the monarch of the main:
> The sea subsiding spreads a level plain:
> The curling waves before his coursers fly:
> The parting surface leaves his brazen axle dry.

BESIDES the metaphors, similes, and allusions of Poetry, there is an infinite variety of tropes, or turns of expression, occasionally disseminated through works of Genius, which serve to animate the whole, and distinguish the glowing effusions of real inspiration from the cold efforts of mere Science.   These tropes consist of a certain happy choice and arrangement of words, by which ideas are artfully disclosed in a great variety of attitudes; of epithets, and compound epithets; of sounds collected in order to echo the sense conveyed; of apostrophes; and above all, the enchanting use of the profopopœia, which is a kind of magic, by which the Poet gives life and motion to every inanimate part of .Nature. Homer, defcribing the wrath of Agamemnon, in the firft book of the Iliad, ftrikes off a glowing image in two words:

—— ὅσσι δ'οἱ πυρὶ λαμπιτόυντι ἴιχτην.

—And from his eye-balls *flafh'd the living fire.*

This, indeed, is a figure which has been copied by Virgil, and almoft all the Poets of every age—*oculis* micat *acribus ignis*—ignefcunt iræ : *auris dolor offibus* ardet. Milton defcribing Satan in Hell, fays,

With head uplift above the wave, and eye
That *fparkling blaz'd !—*

—He fpake : and to confirm his words out flew
Millions of flaming fwords, drawn from the thighs
Of mighty cherubims. The fudden *blaze*
Far round *illumin'd* Hell—

There are certain words in every language particularly adapted to Poetical expreffion ; fome from the image or idea they convey to the imagination ; and fome from the effect they have upon the ear. The firft are truly *figurative* ; the others may be called *emphatical.—*Rollin obferves,

that

that Virgil has upon many occafions Poetized
(if we may be allowed the expreffion) a whole
fentence by means of the fame word, which is
pendere.

> *Ite meæ, felix quondam pecus, ite capellæ.*
> *Non ego vos pofthac viridi projectu: in antro*
> *Dumofa pendere procul de rupe videbo.*

> At eafe reclin'd beneath the verdant fhade,
> No more fhall I behold my happy flock
> Aloft *hang* brouzing on the tufted rock.

Here the word *pendere* wonderfully improves the
landfcape, and renders the whole paffage beauti-
fully picturefque. The fame figurative verb we
meet with in many different parts of the Æneid.

> *Hi fummo in fluctu* pendent, *his unda* dehifcens
> *Terram inter fluctus aperit.*

> Thefe on the mountain billow *hung:* to thofe
> The *yawning waves* the yellow fand difclofe.

In this inftance, the words *pendent* and *dehifcens,*
hung and *yawning*, are equally Poetical. Addi-
fon feems to have had this paffage in his eye,
when he wrote his Hymn which is inferted in the
Spectator :

> —For though in dreadful whirle we *hung*,
> High on the broken wave.

K 2

And

And in another piece of a like nature, in the same collection :

> Thy Providence my life fuftain'd
> And all my wants redreft,
> When in the filent womb I lay,
> And *bung* upon the breaft.

Shakefpeare, in his admired defcription of Dover cliff, ufes the fame expreffion :

> —half way down
> *Hangs* one that gathers famphire, dreadful trade !

NOTHING can be more beautiful than the following picture, in which Milton hath introduced the fame expreffive tint :

> —he, on his fide,
> Leaning half rais'd, with looks of cordial love
> *Hung* over her enamour'd———

WE fhall give cne example more from Virgil, to fhew in what a variety of fcenes it may appear with propriety and effect. In defcribing the progrefs of Dido's paffion for Æneas, the Poet fays,

> *Iliacos iterum demens audire labores*
> *Expofcit,* pendetque *iterum narrantis ab ore.*

> The woes of Troy once more fhe begg'd to hear ;
> Once more the mournful tale employ'd his tongue,
> While in fond rapture on his lips fhe *bung*.

THE

THE reader will perceive in all thefe inftances, that no other word could be fubftituted with equal energy ; indeed, no other word could be ufed without degrading the fenfe, and defacing the image.

THERE are many other verbs of Poetical im-port, fetched from Nature and from Art, which the Poet ufes to advantage both in a literal and metaphorical fenfe ; and thefe have been always tranflated for the fame purpofe from one language to another : fuch as *quaffo, concutio, cio, fufcito, lenio, fævio, mano, fluo, ardeo, mico, aro,* to fhake, to wake, to roufe, to foothe, to rage, to flow, to fhine or blaze, to plough.—Quaffantia *tectum limina Æneas, cafu concuffus acerbo— Ære* ciere *viros, martemque accendere cantu— Æneas acuit martem & fe* fufcitat *ira—Impium* lenite *clamorem.* Lenibant *curas—Ne* fævi *mag-na facerdos—Sudor ad imos* manabat *folos—Suf-penfæque diu lachrymæ* fluxere *per ora—Juvenali* ardebat *amore—*Micat *æreus enfis—Nullum ma-ris æquor* arandum. It will be unneceffary to in-fert examples of the fame nature from the En-glifh Poets.

THE words we term *emphatical,* are fuch as by their found exprefs the fenfe they are intended

K 3   to

to convey ; and with thefe the Greek abounds,
above all other languages, not only from its natural copioufnefs, flexibility, and fignificance, but
alfo from the variety of its Dialects, which enables
a writer to vary his terminations occafionally as the
nature of the fu ject requires, without offending
the moft delicate ear, or incurring the imputation
of adopting vulgar provincial expreffions. Every
fmatterer in Gr ek can repeat

Βῆ δ' ἀκέων παρὰ θῖνα πολυφλοσβοιο θαλασσης,

in which the two laft words wonderfully echo to
the fenfe, conveying the idea of the fea dafhing
on the fhore. How much more fignificant in
found than that beautiful image of Shakefpeare—

" The fea that on th' unnumber'd pebbles beats."

And yet, if we confider the ftrictnefs of propriety, this laft expreffion would feem to have
been felected on purpofe to concur with the other
circumftances which are brought together to afcertain the vaft height of Dover cliff : for the Poet
adds, ' cannot be heard fo high.' The place
where Glofter ftood was fo high above the furface of the fea, that the φλοιςβος, or *dafhing*, could
not be heard ; and therefore an enthufiaftic ad-
mirer of Shakefpeare might with fome plaufibility
affirm, the Poet had chofen an expreffion in which
that found is not at all conveyed.

IN

In the very fame page of Homer's Iliad, we meet with two other ftriking inftances of the fame fort of beauty. Apollo, incenfed at the infults his prieft had fuftained, defcends from the top of Olympus, with his bow and quiver rattling on his fhoulder as he moved along :

"Εκλαγξαν δ' αρ' οισω επ' ωμων.

Here the found of the word "Εκλαγξαν admirably expreffes the clanking of armour ; as the third line after this furprifingly imitates the twanging of a bow.

Δεινη δε κλαγγη γενετ' αργυρεοιο βιοιο.

In fhrill ton'd murmurs fung the twanging bow.

MANY beauties of the fame kind are fcattered through Homer, Pindar, and Theocritus, fuch as the βομβευσα μελισσα, *fufurrans apicula* ; the αδυ ψιθυρισμα, *dulcem fufurrum* ; and the μελισδεται for the fighing of the pine.

THE Latin language teems with founds adapted to every fituation, and the Englifh is not deftitute of this fignificant energy. We have the *cooing* turtle, the *fighing* reed, the *warbling* rivulet, the *fliding* ftream, the *whifpering* breeze, the glance, the gleam, the flafh, the *bickering* flame, the

K 4   *dafhing*

dafhing wave, the *gufhing* fpring, the *howling* bl..t, the *rattling* ftorm, the *pattering* fhower, the *crimp* earth, the *mould ring* tower, the *twanging* bow-ftring, the *clanging* arms, the *clanking* chains, the *twinkling* ftars, the *tinkling* chords, the *trickling* drops, the *twittering* fwallow, the *cawing* rook, the *fcreeching* owl; and a thoufand other words and epithets wonderfully fuited to the fenfe they imply.

AMONG the felect paffages of Poetry which we fhall infert by way of illuftration, the reader will find inftances of all the different tropes and figures, which the beft authors have adopted in the variety of their Poetical works, as well as of the apoftrophe, abrupt tranfition, repetition, and profopopœia.

IN the mean time, it will be neceffary ftill further to analyfe thofe principles which conftitute the effence of Poetical merit; to difplay thofe delightful parterres that teem with the faireft flowers of imagination, and diftinguifh between the gaudy offspring of a cold infipid fancy, and the glowing progeny, diffufing fweets, produced and invigorated by the Sun of Genius.

K 4   E S S A Y

E S S A Y   XVII.

OF all the implements of Poetry, the Metaphor is the moſt generally and ſuccefsfully uſed, and indeed may be termed the Muſe's Caduceus, by the power of which ſhe enchants all Nature. The Metaphor is a ſhorter ſimile, or rather a kind of magical coat, by which the ſame idea aſſumes a thouſand different appearances. Thus the word *plough*, which originally belongs to agriculture, being metaphorically uſed, repreſents the motion of a ſhip at ſea, and the effects of old age upon the human countenance—

—Plough'd the boſom of the deep—
And time had plough'd his venerable front.

ALMOST every verb, noun ſubſtantive, or term of art in any language, may be in this manner applied to a variety of ſubjects with admirable effect ; but the danger is in ſowing metaphors too thick, ſo as to diſtract the imagination of the reader, and incur the imputation of deſerting Na-

K 5   ture,

ture, in order to hunt after conceits. Every day produces Poems of all kinds fo inflated with metaphor, that they may be compared to the gaudy bubbles blown up from a folution of foap. Longinus is of opinion, that a multitude of metaphors is never excufable; except in thofe cafes when the paffions are roufed, and, like a winter torrent, rufh down impetuous, fweeping them with collective force along. He brings an inftance of the following quotation from Demofthenes. "Men! (fays he) profligates, mifcreants, and flatterers, who, having feverally preyed upon the bowels of their country, at length betrayed her liberty, firft to Philip, and now again to Alexander; who, placing the chief felicity of life in the indulgence of infamous lufts and appetites, overturned in the duft that freedom and independence, which was the chief aim and end of all our worthy anceftors——*."

ARISTOTLE and Theophraftus feem to think it is rather too bold and hazardous to ufe metaphors

* "Ανθρωποι, φησι, μιαροι, και ολασορες, και κολακες, ηκρωτηριασμενοι τας εαυτων εκασοι πατριδας, την ελευθεριαν προπεπωκοτες, προτερον Φιλιππω, νυν δ'Αλεξανδρω, τη γαςρι μετρουντες και τοις αισχισοις την ευδαιμονιαν, την δ'ελευθεριαν, και το μηδενα εχειν δεσποτην αιτων, α τοις προτεροις, Ελλησιν οσοι των αγαθων ησαν και κανονες, &c. &c."

fo

fo freely, without interpofing fome mitigating phrafe ; fuch as, " if I may be allowed the ex- preffion," or fome equivalent excufe. At the fame time, Longinus finds fault with Plato for hazard- ing fome metaphors which indeed appear to be equally affected and extravagant, when he fays, " the government of a ftate fhould not refemble a bowl of hot fermenting wine, but a cool and mode- rate beverage, *chaftifed by the fober deity*"—a me- taphor that fignifies nothing more than " mixed or lowered with water." Demetrius Phalereus juftly obferves, that though a judicious ufe of me- taphors wonderfully raifes, fublimes, and adorns oratory or elocution; yet they fhould feem to flow naturally from the fubject ; and too great a re- dundancy of them inflates tne difcourfe to a mere rhapfody. The fame obfervation will hold in Poe- try ; and the more liberal or fparing ufe of them will depend in a great meafure on the nature of the fubject.

PASSION itfelf is very figurative, and often burfts out into metaphors ; but, in touching the pathos, the Poet muft be perfectly well acquainted with the emotions of the human foul, and carefully dif- tinguifh between thofe metaphors which rife glow- ing from the heart, and thofe cold con.cits which are ingendered in the fancy. Should one of thefe

K 6   laft

laft unfortunately intervene, it will be apt to deftroy
the whole effect of the moft pathetical incident or
fituation. Indeed it requires the moft delicate
Tafte, and a confummate knowledge of propriety,
to employ metaphors in fuch a manner, as to
avoid what the Antients called the τὸ ψυχρὸν, the
frigid, or falfe fublime. Inftances of this kind
were frequent even among the correct Antients.
Sappho herfelf is blamed for ufing the hyperbole
λευκοτεροι χιόνος, *whiter than fnow*. Demetrius is
fo nice as to be difgufted at the fimile of *fwift as*
the wind; though, in fpeaking of a race-horfe,
we know from experience that this is not even
an byperbole. He would have had more reafon
to cenfure that kind of metaphor which Ariftotle
ftiles κατ' ἐνέργειαν, exhibiting things inanimate as
endued with fenfe and reafon ; fuch as that of the
fharp-pointed arrow *eager* to take wing among the
crowd. " Ο' ξυβελὴς καθ' ὅμιλον ἐπιπτέσθαι μενεαίνων."
Not but that in defcriptive Poetry this figure is
often allowed and admired. The *cruel* fword,
the *ruthlefs* dagger, the *ruffian* blaft, are epithets
which frequently occur. The *faithful* bofom of
the earth ; the *joyous* boughs ; the trees that *ad-*
mire their images reflected in the ftream ; and
many other examples of this kind, are found dif-
feminated through the works of our beft modern
Poets : yet ftill they muft be fheltered under the
privilege

privilege of the *poetica licentia* ; and, except in Poetry, they would give offence.

MORE chaste metaphors are freely used in all kinds of writing ; more sparingly in History, and more abundantly in Rhetoric: we have seen that Plato indulges them even to excess. The orations of Demosthenes are animated, and even inflamed with metaphors, some of them so bold as even to entail upon him the censure of the critics. Τότι τῷ Πυθωνι τω ῥήτορι ῥίοντι καθ᾽ ὑμῶν---"then I did not yield to Python the orator, when he *overflowed* you with a tide of eloquence." Cicero is still more liberal in the use of them ; he ransacks all nature, and pours forth a redundancy of figures, even with a lavish hand. Even the chaste Xenophon, who generally illustrates his subject by way of simile, sometimes ventures to produce an expressive metaphor, such as " part of the phalanx *fluctuated* in the march; and indeed nothing can be more significant than this word ἰξικύμηνι, to represent a body of men staggered, and on the point of giving way. Armstrong has used the word *fluctuate* with admirable efficacy, in his Philosophical Poem entituled *The Art of Preserving Health*.

> O ! when the growling winds contend, and all
> The founding forest *fluctuates* in the storm,
> To sink in warm repose, and hear the din
> Howl o'er the steady battlements——

THE word *fluctuate* on this occafion not only exhibits an idea of ftruggling, but alfo echoes to the fenfe, like the εφριξεν δὲ μαχη of Homer ; which, by the bye, it is impoffible to render into Englifh : for the verb φρισσω fignifies not only to ftand erect like prickles, as a grove of lances, but alfo to make a noife like the crafhing of armour, the hiffing of javelins, and the fplinters of fpears.

OVER and above an excefs of Figures, a young author is apt to run into a confufion of mixed metaphors, which leave the fenfe disjointed, and diftract the imagination : Shakefpeare himfelf is often guilty of thefe irregularities. The Soliloquy, in Hamlet, which we have fo often heard extolled in terms of admiration, is, in our opinion, a . heap of abfurdities, whether we confider the fituation, the fentiment, the argumentation, or the Poetry. Hamlet is informed by the Ghoft, that his father was murdered, and therefore he is tempted to murder himfelf, even after he had promifed to take vengeance on the ufurper, and exprefled the utmoft eagernefs to atchieve this enterprize. It does not appear that he had the leaft reafon to wifh for death ; but every motive which may be fuppofed to influence the mind of a young Prince concurred to render life defirable — re-
.venge

venge towards the ufurper ; love for the fair Ophe-
lia ; and the ambition of reigning. Befides,
when he had an opportunity of dying without being acceffary to his own death ; when he had nothing to do but, in obedience to his uncle's command, to allow himfelf to be conveyed quietly
to England, where he was fure of fuffering dea·h ;
inftead of amufing himfelf with meditations on
mortality, he very wifely confulted the means of·
felf-prefervation, turned the tables upon his attendants, and returned to Denmark   But granting him to have been reduced to the loweft ftate
of defpondence, furrounded with nothing but horror and defpair, fick of this life, and eager to tempt
futurity, we fhall fee how far he argues like a
Philofopher.

IN order to fupport this general charge againft
an author fo univerfally held in veneration, whofe
very errors have helped to fanctify his character
among the Multitude, we will defcend to particulars, and analyfe this famous Soliloquy.

HAMLET, having affumed the difguife of madnefs, as a cloak under which he might the more
effectually revenge his father's death upon the
murderer and ufurper, appears alone upon the
ftage in a penfive and melancholy attitude, and
communes with himfelf in thefe words :

To

To be, or not to be ? That is the queſtion.
Whether 'tis nobler in the mind, to ſuffer
The ſlings and arrows of outrageous fortune,
Or to take arms againſt a ſea of troubles,
And by oppoſing, end them ?—To die—to ſleep—
No more ; and by a ſleep, to ſay, we end
The heart-ach, and the thouſand natural ſhocks
That fleſh is heir to ; 'tis a conſummation
Devoutly to be wiſh'd.—To die—to ſleep—
To ſleep ! perchance to dream ; ay, there's the rub—
For in that ſleep of death what dreams may come,
When we have ſhuffled off this mortal coil,
Muſt give us pauſe.——There's the reſpeſt
That makes calamity of ſo long life.
For who would bear the whips and ſcorns of time,
Th' oppreſſor's wrong, the proud man's contumely,
The pangs of deſpiſed love, the law's delay,
The inſolence of office, and the ſpurns
That patient merit of th' unworthy takes,
When he himſelf might his *quietus* make
With a bare bodkin ? Who would fardles bear,
To groan and ſweat under a weary life,
But that the dread of ſomething after death
(That undiſcover'd country, from whoſe bourne
No traveller returns) puzzles the will;
And makes us rather bear thoſe ills we have,
Than fly to others that we know not of.
Thus conſcience does make cowards of us all ;
And thus the native hue of reſolution
Is ſicklied o'er with the pale caſt of thought ;
And enterprizes of great pith and moment,
With this regard, their currents turn away,
And loſe the name of aſtion.

WE

WE have already obferved, that there is not any apparent circumftance in the fate or fituation of Hamlet, that fhould prompt him to harbour one thought of felf murder ; and therefore thefe ex- preffions of defpair imply an impropriety in point of character. But fuppofing his condition was truly defperate, and he faw no poffibility of re- pofe but in the uncertain harbour of death, let us fee in what manner he argues on the fubject. The queftion is, " To be, or not to be ;" to die by my own hand, or live and fuffer the miferies of life. He proceeds to explain the alternative in thefe terms, " Whether 'tis nobler in the mind to fuffer, or endure the frowns of fortune, or to take arms, and by oppofing, end them." Here he deviates from his firft propofition, and death is no longer the queftion. The only doubt is, whether he will ftoop to misfortune, or exert his faculties in order to furmount it. This furely is the obvious meaning, and indeed the only mean- ing that can be implied in thefe words,

> Whether 'tis nobler in the mind to fuffer
> The flings and arrows of outrageous fortune,
> Or to take arms againft a fea of troubles,
> And by oppofing, end them.

HE now drops this idea, and reverts to his rea- foning on death, in the courfe of which he owns
himfelf

himfelf deterred from fuicide by the thoughts of what may follow death ;

> ──the dread of fomething after death
> (That undifcover'd country, from whofe bourne
> No traveller returns).

THIS might be a good argument in a Heathen or Pagan, and fuch indeed Hamlet really was ; but Shakefpeare has already reprefented him as a good Catholic, who muft have been acquainted with the truths of revealed religion, and fays exprefsly in this very play,

> ──had not the Everlafting fix'd
> His canon 'gainft felf-murder.

MOREOVER, he had juft been converfing with his father's Spirit piping hot from purgatory, which we prefume is not within the *bourne* of this world. The dread of what may happen after death (fays he)

> Makes us rather bear thofe *ills* we have,
> Than fly to *others* that we know not of.

THIS declaration at leaft implies fome knowledge of the other world, and exprefsly afferts, that there muft be *ills* in that world, though what kind of *ills* they are, we do not know. The argument

gument therefore may be reduced to this lemma :
This world abounds with *ills* which I feel : the
other world abounds with *ills*, the nature of which
I do not know : therefore, I will rather bear
thofe *ills* I have, than fly to *others* which I know
not of :" a deduction amounting to a certainty,
with refpect to the only circumftance that could
create a doubt, namely, whether in death he
fhould reft from his mifery ; and if he was certain
there were evils in the next world, as well as in
this, he had no room to reafon at all about the
matter. What alone could juftify his thinking on
this fubject, would have been the hope of flying
from the ills of this world, without encountering
any *others* in the next.

NOR is Hamlet more accurate in the following
reflection :

Thus confcience does make cowards of us all.

A BAD confcience will make us cowards ; but
a good confcience will make us brave. It does
not appear that any thing lay heavy on his confcience ; and from the premifes we cannot help
inferring that confcience in this cafe was entirely
out of the queftion. Hamlet was deterred from
fuicide by a full conviction, that in flying from
one fea of troubles which he did know, he fhould
fall into *another* which he did not know.

His

His whole chain of reafoning, therefore, feems
inconfiftent and incongruous. " I am doubtful
whether I fhould live,or do violence upon my own
life : for I know not whether it is more honourable
to bear misfortune patiently, than to exert myfclf
in oppofing misfortune, and by oppofing, end it."
Let us throw it into the form of a fyllogifm, it
will ftand thus : " I am oppreffed with ills : I
know not whether it is more honourable to bear
thofe ills patiently, or to end them by taking arms
againft them ; *ergo*, I am doubtful whether I
fhould flay myfelf or live.   To die, is no more
than to fleep ; and to *fay* that by a fleep we end
the heart-ach, &c. 'tis a confummation devoutly
to be wifh'd."   Now, to *fay it*, was of no confequence unlefs it had been true. " I am afraid of the
dreams that may happen in that fleep of death ;
and I choofe rather to bear thofe ills I have in this
life, than fly to *other ills* in that undifcovered
country from whofe bourne no traveller returns.
I have ills that are almoft infupportable in this
life.   I know not what is in the next, becaufe it
is an undifcovered country :   *ergo*, I'd rather
bear thofe ills I have, than fly to others which I
know not of."   Here the conclufion is by no
means warranted by the premifes. . " I am fore
afflicted in this life : but, I will rather bear the
afflictions of this life, than plunge myfelf in the
                                                    afflictions

afflictions of another life : *ergo*, confcience makes cowards of us all." But this conclufion would juftify the logician in faying, *negatur confequens*; for it is entirely detached both from the major and minor propofition.

THIS Soliloquy is not lefs unexceptionable in the propriety of expreffion, than in the chain of argumentation.—" To die,—to fleep - no more," contains an ambiguity which all the art of punctuation cannot remove ; for it may fignify that " to die, is to fleep no more ;" or the expreffion—" no more," may be confidered as an abrupt apoftrophe in thinking, as if he meant to fay—" no more of that reflection."

" Ay, there's the rub"—is a vulgarifm beneath the dignity of Hamlet's character, and the words that follow leave the fenfe imperfect ;

> For in that fleep of death, what dreams may come,
> When we have fhuffled off this mortal coil,
> Muft give us paufe.

Not the dreams that might come, but, the fear of what dreams' might come, occafioned the paufe or hefitation. *Refpect*, in the fame line, may be allowed to pafs for confideration : but,

> Th' oppreffor's wrong, the proud man's contumely,

according to the invariable acceptation of the words *wrong* and *contumely*, can fignify nothing but

but the wrongs fuſtained by the oppreſſor, and the contumely or abuſe thrown upon the proud man ; though it is plain that Shakeſpeare uſed them in a different ſenſe : neither is the word *ſpurn* a ſubſtantive ; yet as ſuch he has inſerted it in theſe lines :

> The inſolence of office, and the ſpurns
> That patient merit of the unworthy takes.

IF we conſider the metaphors of this Soliloquy, we ſhall find them jumbled together in ſtrange confuſion.

IF the metaphors were reduced to Painting, we ſhould find it a very difficult taſk, if not altogether impracticable, to repreſent with any propriety outrageous Fortune uſing her ſlings and arrows, between which, indeed, there is no ſort of analogy in Nature. Neither can any figure be more ri- diculouſly abſurd than that of a man taking arms againſt a ſea, excluſive of the incongruous med- ley of ſlings, arrows, and ſeas, juſtled within the compaſs of one reflection. What follows is a ſtrange rhapſody of broken images, of ſleeping, dreaming, and ſhifting off a *coil*, which laſt con- veys no idea that can be repreſented on canvas. A man may be exhibited ſhuffling off his garments or his chains : but how he ſhould ſhuffle off a *coil*,

which

which is another term for noife and tumult, we
cannot comprehend.   Then we have " long-lived
Calamity," and "Time armed with whips and
fcorns ;" and "patient Merit fpurned at by Unwor-
thinefs ;" and " Mifery with a bare bodkin going
to make his own *quietus*," which, at beft, is but a
mean metaphor.   Thefe are followed by Figures
" fweating under fardles of burdens," " puzzled
with doubts," " fhaking with fears," and " flying
from evils." Finally, we fee " Refolution ficklied
o'er with pale thought," a conception like that of
reprefenting health by ficknefs ; and a "current of
pith turned away fo as to lofe the name of action,"
which is both an error in fancy, and a folecifm in
fenfe. In a word, this Soliloquy may be compared
to the *Ægri fomnia,* and the *Tabula, cujus vanæ
fingentur fpecies.*

BUT while we cenfure the chaos of broken,
incongruous metaphors, we ought alfo to caution
the young Poet againft the oppofite extreme of
purfuing a metaphor until the fpirit of it is quite
exhaufted in a fucceffion of cold conceits ; fuch as
we fee in the following letter, faid to be fent by
Tamerlane to the Turkifh Emperor Bajazet.
" Where is the monarch that dares oppofe our
"arms ? Where is the potentate who doth not glory
" in being numbered amongft our vaffals ? As for
" thee, defcended from a Turcoman mariner, fince
" the veffel of thy unbounded ambition hath been
                                              " wrecked

wrecked in the gulph of thy felf-love, it would be
proper that thou fhouldeft furl the fails of thy te-
merity, and caft the anchor of repentance in the
port of fincerity and juftice, which is the harbour
of fafety : left the tempeft of our vengeance
make thee perifh in the fea of that punifhment
thou haft deferved."

But if thefe laboured conceits are ridiculous in
Poetry, they are ftill more inexcufable in Profe :
fuch as we find them frequently occur in Strada's
Bellum Belgicum. *Vix defcenderat à prætoria
navi Cæfar ; cùm fæda illico exorta in portu tem-
peftas, claffem impetu disjecit, prætoriam haufit;
quafi non vecturam amplius Cæfarem Cæfarifque
fortunam.* " Cæfar had fcarce fet his feet on fhore,
when a terrible tempeft arifing, fhattered the fleet
even in the harbour, and fent to the bottom the
P"æ'orian fhip, as if refolved it fhould no longer
carry Cæfar and his fortunes."

Yet this is modeft in comparifon of the following flowers : *Alii, pulfis è tormento catenis dif-
cerpti fectique, dimidiato corpore pugnabant fibi fu-
perftites, ac peremptæ partis ultoris.* "Others, dif-
fevered and cut in twain by chain-fhot, fought
with one half of their bodies that remained, in revenge of the other half that was flain."

HOMER

HOMER, Horace, and even the chaſte Virgil, is not free from conceits. The latter, ſpeaking of a man's hand cut off in battle, ſays,

Te decifa fuum, Laride, dextera quærit :
Semianimefque micant digiti, ferrumque retractant :

thus enduing the amputated hand with ſenſe and volition. This, to be ſure, is a violent figure, and hath been juſtly condemned by ſome accurate critics : but we think they are too ſevere in extending the ſame cenſure to ſome other paſſages in the moſt admired authors.

VIRGIL in his Sixth Eclogue, ſays,

Omnia quæ, Phœbo quondam meditante, beatus
Audiit Eurotas, juſſitque ediſcere lauros,
Ille canit.

Whate'er when Phœbus bleſs'd th' Arcadian plain,
Eurotas heard and taught his bays the ſtrain,
The ſenior ſung—

And Pope has copied the conceit in his Paſtorals,

Thames heard the numbers as he flow'd along,
And bade his willows learn the mournng ſong.

VIDA thus begins his Firſt Eclogue :

Dicite, vos muſæ, et juvenum memorate querelas ;
Dicite : nam motas ipſas ad carmina cautes,
Et requiéſſe ſuos perhibent vaga flumina curſus.

Say heav'nly mufe, their youthful frays rehearfe ;
Begin, ye daughters of immortal verfe ;
Exulting rocks have own'd the power of fong,
And rivers liften'd as they flow'd along—

RACINE adopts the fame bold figure in his
Phædra:

Le flot qui l'apporta recule epouvanté:

The wave that bore him, backwards fhrunk appall'd.

EVEN Milton has indulged himfelf in the fame
licence of expreffion—

—As when to them who fail
Beyond the Cape of Hope, and now are paft
Mozambic, off at fea north-eaft winds blow
Sabæan odour from the fpicy fhore
Of Araby the bleft ; with fuch delay
Well pleas'd, they flack their courfe, and many a league
Chear'd with the grateful fmell, old ocean fmiles.

SHAKESPEARE fays,

———I've feen
'Th' ambitious ocean fwell, and rage, and foam,
To be exalted with the threat'ning clouds.

AND indeed more correct writers, both ancient and modern, abound with the fame kind of
figure, which is reconciled to propriety, and even
invefted with beauty, by the efficacy of the profopopœia,

pœia, which perfonifies the object. Thus, when Virgil fays Enipeus heard the fongs of Apollo, he raifes up, as by enchantment, the idea of a river god crowned with fedges, his head raifed above the ftream, and in his countenance the expreffion of pleafed attention. By the fame magic we fee in the couplet quoted from Pope's Paftorals, old father Thames leaning upon his urn, and liftening to the Poet's ftrain.

THUS in the regions of Poetry, all Nature, even the paffions and affections of the mind, may be perfonified into picturefque figures for the entertainment of the reader. Ocean fmiles or frowns, as the fea is calm or tempeftuous ; a Triton rules on every angry billow ; every mountain has its Nymph ; every ftream its Naiad ; every tree its Hamydryad ; and every art its Genius. We cannot therefore affent to thofe who cenfure Thomfon as licentious for ufing the following figure :

O vale of blifs ! O foftly fwelling hills !
On which the power of cultivation lies,
And joys to fee the wonders of his toil.

WE cannot conceive a more beautiful image than that of the Genius of Agriculture diftinguifhed by the implements of his art, imbrown'd with labour, glowing with health, crowned with a garland of foliage, flowers, and fruit, lying ftretched at his eafe on the brow of a gentle fwelling hill, and contemplating with pleafure the happy effects of his own induftry.

NEITHER can we join iffue againft Shakefpeare for this comparifon, which hath likewife incurred the cenfure of the Critics :

——The noble fifter of Poplicola,
The moon of Rome; chafte as the icicle
That's curdled by the froft from pureft fnow,
And hangs on Dian's temple—

This is no more than illuftrating a quality of the mind, by comparing it with a fenfible object. If there is no impropriety in faying fuch a man is true as fteel, firm as a rock, inflexible as an oak, unfteady as the ocean, or in defcribing a difpofition cold as ice, or fickle as the wind ; and thefe expreffions are juftified by conftant practice ; we fhall hazard an affertion, that the comparifon of a chafte woman to an icicle is proper and picturefque, as it obtains only in the circumftances of cold and purity ; but that the addition of its being curdled from the pureft fnow, and hanging on the temple of Diana, the patronefs of virginity, heightens the whole into a moft beautiful fimile,

that

that gives a very refpectable and amiable idea of the character in queftion.

THE Simile is no more than an extended metaphor introduced to illuftrate and beautify the fubject: it ought to be apt, ftriking, properly purfued, and adorned with all the graces of Poetical melody. But a fimile of this kind ought never to proceed from the mouth of a perfon under any great agitation of fpirit ; fuch as a tragic character overwhelmed with grief, diftracted by contending cares, or agonifing in the pangs of death. The language of paffion will not admit fimile, which is always the refult of ftudy and deliberation. We will not allow a hero the privilege of a dying fwan, which is faid to chant its approaching fate in the moft melodious ftrain ; and therefore nothing can be more ridiculoufly unnatural, than the reprefentation of a lover dying upon the ftage with a laboured fimile in his mouth.

THE orientals, whofe language was extremely figurative, have been very carelefs in the choice of their fimilies : provided the refemblance obtained in one circumftance, they minded not whether they difagreed with the fubject in every other refpect. Many inftances of this defect in congruity, may be culled from the moft fublime parts of Scripture.

L. 3   HOMER

HOMER has been blamed for the bad choice of his fimiles on fome particular occafions. He compares Ajax to an afs, in the Iliad, and Ulyffes to a fteak broiling on the coals, in the Odyffey. His admirers have endeavoured to excufe him, by reminding us of the fimplicity of the age in which he wrote ; but they have not been able to prove that any ideas of dignity or importance were, even in thofe days, affixed to the character of an afs, or the quality of a beef-collop ; therefore, they were very improper illuftrations for any fituation in which a hero ought to be reprefented.   ˎ

VIRGIL has degraded the wife of king Latinus by comparing her, when fhe was actuated by the fury, to a top which the boys lafh for diverfion. This, doubtlefs, is a low image, though in other refpects the comparifon is not deftitute of propriety ; but he is much more juftly cenfured for the following fimile, which has no fort of reference to the fubject. Speaking of Turnus he fays,

——*medio dux agmine Turnus*
Vertitur arma tenens, et toto vertice fupra eft.
Ceu feptem furgens fedatis amnibus altus
Per tacitum Ganges : aut pingui flumine Nilus,
Cùm refluit campis, et jam fe condidit alveo.

But Turnus, chief amidft the warrior train,
In armour tow'rs the talleft on the plain.

The

The Ganges thus by seven rich streams supply'd,
A mighty mass devolves in silent pride.
Thus Nilus pours from his prolific urn,
When from the fields o'erflow'd his vagrant streams return.

These, no doubt, are majestic images; but they bear no sort of resemblance to an hero glittering in armour at the head of his forces.

HORACE has been ridiculed by some shrewd critics for this comparison, which, however, we think is more defensible than the former. Addressing himself to Munatius Plancus, he says:

Albus ut obscuro deterget nubila cælo
   Sæpe Notus, neque parturit imbres
Perpetuos : sic tu sapiens finire memento
   Tristitiam, vitæque labores
Molli, Plance, mero.——

As Notus often, when the welkin low'rs,
Sweeps off the clouds, nor teems perpetual show'rs,
So let thy wisdom, free from anxious strife,
In mellow wine dissolve the cares of life.

                         DUNKIN.

The analogy, it must be confessed, is not very striking : but, nevertheless, it is not altogether void of propriety. The Poet reasons thus : As the South-wind, though generally attended with rain, is often known to dispel the clouds, and ren-

                             der

der the weather ferene ; fo do you, though gene.
rally on the rack of thought, remember to relax
fometimes, and drown your cares in wine. As-
the South-wind is not always moift, fo you ought
not always to be dry,

A FEW inftances of inaccuracy, or mediocrity,
can never derogate from the fuperlative merit of
Homer and Virgil, whofe Poems are the great
magazines, replete with every fpecies of beauty
and magnificence, particularly abounding with
fimiles which aftonifh, delight, and tranfport the
reader.

EVERY fimile ought not only to be well adapted
to the fubject, but alfo to include every excellence
of defcription, and to be coloured with the
warmeft tints of Poetry.   Nothing can be more
happily hit off than the following in the Georgics,
to which the Poet compares Orpheus lamenting
his loft Eurydice.

Qualis populeâ mœrens Philomela fub umbrâ
Amiffos queritur fœtus, quos durus arator
Obfervans nido implumes detraxit ; at illa
Flet noctem, ramoque fedens miferabile carmen
Integrat, et mœftis latè loca queftibus implet.

So Philomela, from th' umbrageous wood
In ftrains melodious mourns her tender brood,

Snatch'd

Snatch'd from the neft by fome rude ploughman's hand,
On fome lone bough the warbler takes her ftand ;
The live-long night fhe mourns the cruel wrong ;
And hill and dale refound the plaintive fong.

Here we not only find the moft fcrupulous propriety, and the happieft choice, in comparing the
Thracian bard to Philomel the Poet of the grove;
but alfo the moft beautiful defcription, containing
a fine touch of the pathos, in which laft particular, indeed, Virgil, in our opinion, excels all
other Poets, whether ancient or modern.

ONE would imagine that Nature had exhaufted
itfelf, in order to embellifh the Poems of Homer,
Virgil, and Milton, with fimiles and metaphors.
The firft of thefe very often ufes the comparifon
of the wind, the whirlwind, the hail, the torrent,
to exprefs the rapidity of his combatants : but
when he comes to defcribe the velocity of the immortal horfes that drew the chariot of Juno, he
raifes his ideas to the fubject, and as Longinus
obferves, meafures every leap by the whole breadth
of the horizon.

"Οσσον δ'ηεροειδες ανηρ ιδεν οφθαλμοισιν
"Ημενος εν σκοπιη, λευσσων επι οινοπα ποντον,
Τοσσον επιθρωσκυσι θεων υψηχεες ιπποι.

Far as a watchman from fome rock on high
O'er the wide main extends his boundlefs eye ;

Thro'

Thro' fuch a fpace of air with thund'ring found,
At ev'ry leap th' immortal courfers bound.

The celerity of this goddefs feems to be a favourite idea with the Poet; for in another place
he compares it to the thought of a traveller revolv-
ing in his mind the different places he had feen,
and paffing through them in imagination more
fwift than the lightning flies from eaft to weft.

HOMER's beft fimiles have been copied by Virgil, and almoft every fucceeding Poet, howfoever
they may have varied in the manner of expreffion.
In the third book of the Iliad, Menelaus feeing
Paris, is compared to a hungry lion efpying a
hind or goat.

Ὥστε λέων ἐχάρη μεγάλω ἐπί σώματι κύρσας;
Εὑρών ἢ ἔλαφον κερκον ἢ ἄγριον αἶγα, &c.

So joys the lion, if a branching deer
Or mountain goat his bulky prize appear.
In vain the youths oppofe, the maftifs bay,
The lordly favage rends the panting prey.
Thus fond of vengeance, with a furious bound
In clinging arms he leaps upon the ground.

THE Mantuan bard in the tenth book of the
Æneid, applies the fame fimile to Mezentius,
when he beholds Acron in the battle.

Impaftus

Impaſtus ſtabula alta leo ceu ſæpe peragrans,
(Suadet enim veſana fames) ſi forte fugacem
Conſpexit capream, aut ſurgentem in cornua cervum ;
Gaudet hians immane, comaſque arrexit, et hæret
Viſceribus ſuper accumbens : lavit improba teter
Ora cruor.—

Then as a hungry lion, who beholds
A gameſome goat who friſks about the folds,
Or beamy ſtag that grazes on the plain :
He runs, he roars, he ſhakes his riſing mane ;
He grins and opens wide his greedy jaws,
The prey lies panting underneath his paws ;
He fills his famiſh'd maw, his mouth runs o'er
With unchew'd morſels, while he churns the gore.

DRYDEN.

THE reader will perceive that Virgil has improved the ſimile in one particular, and in another
fallen ſhort of his original.   The deſcription of
the lion ſhaking his mane, opening his hideous
jaws diſtained with the blood of his prey, is great
and picturefque : but on the other hand, he has
omitted the circumſtance of devouring it without being intimidated, or reſtrained by the dogs
and youths that ſurround him ; a circumſtance
that adds greatly to our idea of his ſtrength, intrepidity, and importance.

L 6   ESSAY

OF all the figures in Poetry, that called the Hyperbole is managed with the greateſt difficulty. The Hyperbole is an exaggeration with
which the Muſe is indulged for the better illuſtra-
tion of her ſubjeƈt, when ſhe is warmed into en-
thuſiaſm. Quintilian calls it an ornament of the
bolder kind. Demetrius Phalereus is ſtill more ſevere. He ſays, the Hyperbole is of all forms
of ſpeech the moſt frigid. Μάλιςα δὲ ἡ ὑπερβολὴ
ψυχρότατον παντων ;. but this muſt be underſtood
with ſome grains of allowance. Poetry is animated by the paſſions ; and all the paſſions exag-
gerate. Paſſion itſelf is a magnifying medium.
There are beautiful inſtances of the Hyperbole in
the Scripture, which a reader of ſenſibility cannot read without being ſtrongly affeƈted. The
difficulty lies in chuſing ſuch Hyperboles as the
ſubjeƈt will admit of ; for, according to the defini-
tion of Theophraſtus, the frigid, in ſtyle, is that
which exceeds the expreſſion ſuitable to the ſubject.

ject. The judgement does not revolt against Homer for reprefenting the horfes of Ericthonius
running over the ftanding corn without breaking
off the heads, becaufe the whole is confidered as a
fable, and the north wind is reprefented as their
fire: but the imagination is a little ftartled, when
Virgil, in imitation of this Hyperbole, exhibits Camilla as flying over it without even touching the tops.

Illa vel intacta fegetis per fumma volaret
Gramina ——

THIS elegant author, we are afraid, has, upon
fome other occafions, degenerated into the frigid,
in ftraining to improve upon his great mafter.

HOMER, in the Odyffey, a work which Longinus does not fcruple to charge with bearing the
marks of old age, defcribes a ftorm in which all
the four winds were concerned together.

Σὺν δ' Εὖρός τε, Νοτό; τ' ἔπεσε, Ζέφυρός τε δυσαὴς,
Καὶ Βορέης αἰθρηγενέτης μέγα κῦμα κυλίνδων.

WE know that fuch a contention of contrary
blaſts could not poffibly exift in Nature; for
even in hurricanes, the winds blow alternately
from differents points of the compafs. Neverthelefs, Virgil adopts the defcription, and adds to
its extravagance.

Incubuere

Incubuere mari, totumque e feLibus imis
Una Eurufque, Notufque ruunt, creberq ; procellis
Africus.

Here the winds not only blow together, but they
turn the whole body of the ocean topfy turvy—.

Eaft, weft, and fouth, engage with furious fweep,
And from its loweft bed upturn the foaming deep.

The north wind, however, is ftill more mif-
chievous.———

———*Stridens aquilone procella,*
Velum adverſa ſerit, jluctufque ad ſidera tollit.

The fail then Boreas rends with hideous cry,
And whirls the madd'ning billows to the fky.

THE motion of the fea between Scylla and
Charybdis is ftill more magnified ; and Ætna is
exhibited as throwing out volumes of flame,
which brufh the ftars *. Such exprcffions as
thefe are not intended as. a real reprefentation of
the thing fpecified ; they are defigned to ftrike the
reader's imagination ; but they generally ferve as
marks of the author's finking under his own ideas,

* Speaking of the fiift, he fays,
Tollimur in cælum curvato gurgite et ijdem,
Subducta, ad manes imos dejcendimus, unda—
Of the ether,
Attoilitque globos flammarum, et ſidera lambit.

who,

who, apprehenſive of injuring the greatneſs of his own conception, is hurried into exceſs and extravagance.

QUINTILIAN allows the uſe of Hyperbolc, when words are wanting to expreſs any thing in its juſt ſtrength or due energy : then, he ſays, it is þetter to exceed in expreſſion, than fall ſhort of the conception : but he likewiſe obſerves, that there is no figure or form of ſpeech ſo apt to run into fuſtian. *Nec alia magis via in* καϰοζηλιαι *itur.*

Ir the chaſte Virgil has thus treſpaſſed upon Poetical probability, what can we expeæt from Lucan but Hyperboles even more ridiculouſly extravagant ? He repreſents the winds in conteſt, the ſea in ſuſpence, doubting to which it ſhall give way. He affirms that its motion wou'd nave been ſo violent as to produce a ſecond deluge, had not Jupiter kept it under by the clouds ; and as to the ſhip, during this dreadful uproar, *the ſails touch the clouds, while the keel ſtrikes the ground.*

Nubila tanguntur velis, et terra carina.

THIS image of daſhing water at the ſt_rs, Sir Richard Blackmore has produced in colours truly ridiculous. Deſcribing ſpouting whales in his

Prince

Prince Arthur, he makes the following comparifon :

> Like fome prodigious water-engine made
> To play on heav'n, if fire fhould heav'n invade.

THE great fault in all thefe inftances is a deviation from propriety, owing to the erroneous
judgement of the writer, who, endeavouring to
captivate the admiration with novelty, very often
fhocks the underftanding with extravagance. Of
this nature, is the whole defcription of the Cyclops,
both in the Odyffey of Homer and in the Æneid
of Virgil. It muft be owned, however, that the
Latin Poet, with all his merit, is more apt than
his great original to dazzle us with falfe fire, and
practife upon the imagination with gay conceits,
that will not bear the Critic's examination. There
is not in any of Homer's works now fubfifting
fuch an example of the falfe fublime, as Virgil's
defcription of the thunder bolts forging under the
hammers of the Cyclops.

> *Tres imbris torti radios, tres nubis aquofæ*
> *Addiderant, rutili tres ignis et alitis Auftri.*

> Three rays of writhen rain, of fire three more,
> Of winged fouthern winds, and cloudy ftore,
> As many parts, the dreadful mixture frame.
> DRYDEN.

This

This is altogether a fantaftic piece of affectation, of which we can form no fenfible image, and ferves to chill the fancy, rather than warm the admiration of a judging reader.

EXTRAVAGANT Hyperbole is a weed that grows in great plenty through the works of our admired Shakefpeare. In the following defcription, which hath been much celebrated, one fees he has had an eye to Virgil's thunder-bolts.

O, then I fee queen Mab hath been with you.
She is the fancy's midwife, and fhe comes
In fhape no bigger than an agat-ftone
On the fore-finger of an alderman,
Drawn with a team of little atomies,
Athwart men's nofes as they lie afleep :.
Her waggon fpokes made of long fpinners legs ;
The cover, of the wings of grafshoppers ;
The traces, of the fmalleft fpider's web ;
The collars, of the *moonfhine's watery beams,* &c,

Even in defcribing fantaftic beings, there is a propriety to be obferved ; but furely nothing can be more revolting to common fenfe, than this numbering of the *moon beams* among the other implements of queen Mab's harnefs, which, though extremely flender and diminutive, are, neverthelefs, objects of the touch, and may be conceived capable of ufe.

THE

THE Ode and Satire admit of the boldeſt Hyperboles : ſuch exaggerations ſuit the impetuous warmth of the one ; and in the other have a good effect in expoſing folly, and exciting horror againſt vice. They may be likewiſe ſuccesfully uſed in Comedy, for moving and managing the powers of ridicule.

E S S A Y XIX.

VERSE is an harmonious arrangement of long and ſhort ſyllables, adapted to different kinds of Poetry, and owes its origin entirely to the meaſured cadence, or muſic, which was uſed when the firſt ſongs or hymns were recited. This muſic, divided into different parts, required a regular return of the ſame meaſure, and thus every *ſtrophe*, *antiſtrophe*, or *ſtanza*, con·ained the ſame number of feet. To know what conſtituted the different kinds of rythmical feet among the antients, with reſpect to the number and quantity of their ſyllables, we have nothing to do but to conſult thoſe who have written on grammar and proſody : it is the buſineſs of a ſchoolmaſter rather than the accompliſhment of a Man of Taſte.

VARIOUS eſſays have been made in different countries to compare the characters of antient and modern verſification, and to point out the difference beyond any poſſibility of miſtake. But they

they have made diftinctions where, in fact, there was no difference, and left the criterion un-obferved. They have transferred the name of rhyme to a regular repetition of the fame found at the end of the line, and fet up this vile monotony as the characteriftic of modern verfe, in contradif-tinction to the feet of the antients, which they pretend, the Poetry of modern languages will not admit.

RHYME, from the Greek word Ρυθμος, is no-thing elfe but number, which was eflential to the antient as well as to the modern verfification. As to the jingle of fimilar founds, though it was never ufed by the antients in any regular return in the middle, or at the end of the line, and was by no means deemed eflential to the verfification, yet they did not reject it as a blemifh, where it occur-red without the appearance of conftraint. We meet with it often in the epithets of Homer,—Αργυρτοιο Βιοιο—Ανας Ανδρων Αγαμεμνων—almoft 'the whole firft Ode of Anacreon is what we call rhyme. The following line of Virgil has been admired for the fimilitude of found in the firft two words.

Ors Arethufa tuo ficulis confunditur undis.

RYTH-

RYTHMUS, or number, is certainly effential to verfe, whether in the dead or living languages; and the real difference between the two, is this : The number in antient verfe relates to the feet, and in modern Poetry to the fyllables ; for to affert that modern Poetry has no feet, is a ridiculous abfurdity. The feet that principally enter into the compofition of Greek and Latin verfes, are either of two or three fyllables : thofe of two fyllables are either both long, as the fpondee ; or both fhort, as the pyrrhic ; or one fhort and the other long, as the iambic, or one long and the other fhort, as the trochee. Thofe of three fyllables are the dactyl of one long and two fhort fyllables ; the anapeft, of two fhort and one long; the tribrachium, of three fhort ; and the moloffus, of three long.

FROM the different combinations of thefe feet, reftricted to certain numbers, the antients formed their different kinds of verfes, fuch as the hexameter or heroic, diftinguifhed by fix feet dactyls and fpondees, the fifth being always a dactyl, and the laft a fpondee : *e. g.*

   1   2   3   4   5   6

Principi-is obf-ta, fe-ro medi-cina pa-ratur.

The

The pentameter of five feet, dactyls and spondees, or of six, reckoning two cæsuras.

$$1 \quad 2 \quad 3 \quad 4 \quad 5 \quad 6$$

Cum mala per lon·gas invalu-ere mo-ras.

They had likewife the iambic of three forts, the dimeter, the trimeter, and the tetrameter, and all the different kinds of lyric verfe fpecified in the odes of Sappho, Alcæus, Anacreon, and Horace. Each of thefe was diftinguifhed by the number, as well as by the fpecies of their feet ; fo that they were doubly reftricted. Now, all the feet of the antient poetry are ftill found in the verfification of living languages ; for as cadence was regulated by the ear, it was impoffible for a man to write melodious verfe without naturally falling into the ufe of ancient feet, though, perhaps, he neither knows their meafure nor denomination. Thus, Spenfer, Shakefpeare, Milton, Dryden, Pope, and all our Poets, abound with dactyls, fpondees, trochees, anapefts, &c. which they ufe indifcriminately in all kinds of compofition, whether Tragic, Epic, Paftoral, or Ode, having in this particular greatly the advantage of the antients, who were reftricted to particular kinds of feet in particular kinds of Verfe. If we then are confined with the fetters of what is called rhyme,

they

they were reſtricted to particular ſpecies of feet ; ſo that the advantages and diſadvantages are pretty equally balanced : but, indeed, the Engliſh are more free in this particular, than any other modern nation. They not only uſe Blank-verſe in Tragedy and the Epic, but even in Lyric Poetry. Milton's tranſlation of Horace's Ode to Pyrrha is univerſally known, and generally admired, in our opinion, much above its merit. There is an Ode extant, without Rhyme, addreſſed to Evening, by the late Mr. Collins, much more beautiful ; and Mr. Warton with ſome others have happily ſucceeded in divers occaſional pieces that are free of this reſtraint : but the number, in all of theſe, depends upon the ſyllables, and not upon the feet, which are unlimited.

It is generally ſuppoſed that the genius of the Engliſh language will not admit of Greek or Latin meaſure : but this, we apprehend, is a miſtake owing to the prejudice of education. It is impoſſible that the ſame meaſure, compoſed of the ſame times, ſhould have a good effect upon the ear in one language, and a bad effect in another. The truth is, we have been accuſtomed from our infancy to the numbers of Engliſh Poetry, and the very ſound and ſignification of the words diſpoſes pofes the ear to receive them in a certain manner ; fo that its difappointment muft be attended with a difagreeable fenfation. In imbibing the firft rudiments of education, we acquire, as it were, another ear for the numbers of Greek and Latin Poetry, and this being referved entirely for the founds and fignifications of the words that conftitute thofe dead languages, will not eafily accommodate itfelf to the founds of our vernacular tongue, though conveyed in the fame time and meafure. In a word, Latin and Greek have annexed to them the ideas of the antient meafure from which they are not eafily disjoined. But we will venture to fay, this difficulty might be furmounted by an effort of attention and a little practice ; and in that cafe we fhould, in time, be as well pleafed with Englifh as with Latin hexameters.

SIR PHILIP SIDNEY is faid to have mifcarried in his effays ; but his mifcarriage was no more than that of failing in an attempt to introduce a new fafhion. The failure was not owing to any defect or imperfection in the fcheme, but to the want of tafte, to the irrefolution and ignorance of the public. Without all doubt, the antient meafure, fo different from that of modern Poetry, muft have appeared remarkably uncouth to people in general, who were ignorant of the claffics ;

fics; and nothing but the countenance and perfeverance of the learned could reconcile them to
the alteration. We have feen feveral late fpecimens of Englifh hexameters and fapphics, fo happily compofed, that by attaching them to the idea
of ancient meafure, we found them in all refpects
as melodious and agreeable to the ear, as the
works of Virgil and Anacreon, or Horace.

Though the number of fyllables diftinguifhes
the nature of the Englifh Verfe from that of the
Greek and Latin, it conftitutes neither harmony
grace, nor expreffion. Thefe muft depend upon
the choice of words, the feat of the accent, the
paufe, and the cadence. The accent, or tone,
is underftood to be an elevation or finking of the
voice in reciting: the paufe is a reft that divides
the verfe into two parts, each of them called an
hemiftich. The paufe and accent, in Englifh
Poetry, vary occafionally, according to the meaning of the words; fo that the hemiftich does not
always confift of an equal number of fyllables,
and this variety is agreeable, as it prevents a dull
repetition of regular ftops, like thofe in the
French verfification, every line of which is divided
by a paufe exactly in the middle. The cadence comprehends that Poetical ftyle which ani-

mates every line, that propriety which gives ftrength and expreffion, that numerofity which renders the verfe fmooth, flowing, and harmonious, that fignificancy which marks the paffions, and, in many cafes, makes the found an echo to the fenfe. The Greek and Latin languages, in being copious and ductile, are fufceptible of a vaft variety of cadences which the living languages will not admit : and of thefe a reader of any ear will judge for himfelf.